THE VILLAIN'S GIRL

A FUC ACADEMY STORY

SAMANTHA ALLARD

ACKNOWLEDGMENTS

For all my wonderful readers.

Jess and Devin for offering invaluable advice and editing expertise.

And finally, to Eve Langlais for letting us write in her world.

CHAPTER ONE

What do you call a shifter who can't shift?

A mongrel.

That word still haunted her, even years later. Mongrel.

Rayna Aikawa-Jensen imagined normal human high school wasn't any better. A teenage girl could still be a bitch, even if they didn't sprout fur and howl at the moon. Perhaps if she'd been in mainstream education, she would have been made fun of for her hairstyle, clothing choices, or music preferences. But Rayna went to one of the few shifter-only schools, so she'd been tormented for being a mongrel.

Rayna had been naive and hadn't known what it meant. When she'd asked her parents, they'd told her. A mongrel was a derogatory word some used to describe a shifter born to parents with vastly different animals when that shifter had yet to display their animal form. That was when Rayna understood. If she took after her father, she could call herself a seal shifter. After her mother, a caladrius. Since she'd not transformed into one or the other yet, she couldn't claim she was either. So, she was just a mongrel.

Her parents had assured her that not all shifters had their

first transformation at the same age, and caladrius didn't change until their late teens. Since the women in the Aikawa family inherited from their maternal line, her parents were certain Rayna would inherit her mother's ability to turn into the beautiful snow-white bird by the time she hit sixteen. The process was a lot of mumbo-jumbo, and she couldn't even begin to get her head around the concept.

What she did understand was that she wasn't completely human. She might not be able to transform, but she did have the shifter healing ability. This was made especially clear when she'd been twelve and fallen off her bike into a busy road. An oncoming car hit her with a speed that broke several bones. The pain had knocked her out, and when she woke up, she was in her bed, her dad sitting next to her, holding her hand. He told her that her mum, poised to help her, had noticed Rayna's bones clicking into place. Rayna had completely healed herself.

But her sixteenth birthday came and went, and still, she remained unable to shift. It made no difference to her classmates if she could heal herself. She was still called a mongrel.

Her parents loved her either way, but Rayna hadn't felt like she'd ever be worthy of the Aikawa name or legacy. They were living descendants of the original caladrius, a majestic white bird with the ability to absorb and expel diseases, and they were known for generations as talented healers in Yangzhou, a tiny province in China. While supernatural creatures really didn't need any help in the healing department—unless it was really bad, shifters could heal most things on their own—humans didn't have the same luxury. Rayna's mother, Hiriko, had been expected to continue the family's service to the community.

Rayna's father had a different story. One not quite so legendary yet still full of family obligations. Adam Jensen was one of the sons of Ruth Jensen, the head of the Redfield seal pod in the UK's Lake District. Ruth planned on him playing a part in leading the pod—being the eldest brother meant he was next in line to lead. When he finished university, Ruth allowed him time to take in the sights of the world, with the understanding that he'd soon return to take his place as rightful heir.

No one knew the trajectory of his whole life would change on that trip. That he would find his mate. Her dad joked that the Goddess herself played a part in his meeting Hiriko while backpacking around China.

When they announced their intention to marry, Ruth Jensen had taken it in stride, but the Aikawas had been furious. The pairing tainted their bloodline.

Rayna's failure to become a caladrius gave proof of their misgivings. The offspring of the mismatched pair was an end to the majestic caladrius line. The shame ran deep. The last time she'd seen the Aikawas had been years ago, and she still remembered the sneer on her grandfather's face. *There's the black sheep of the family. An anomaly. Mongrel.*

After high school, Rayna had a choice to make. Pretty much everyone expected her to leave the shifter community and enter the human world. Go to university, earn a degree, get a "normal" job, meet a nice human man to settle down with, and maybe have some normal human kids with him.

But that didn't appeal to her. Regardless of her inability to shift, she was still one of them. Her healing abilities lay testament to that. So, instead of turning her back on the shifter community, she leaned into it. She took criminology courses in Nottingham and applied to the Furry United Coalition's Newbie Academy—FUCN'A for short—with the intention of becoming an agent so she could protect and defend all shifter kind.

At first, she'd been denied admission to the Academy. The rejection letter explained that the agent training was designed for shifters and suggested she consider going into law enforcement on the human side of things. There was even a nice note about how FUC would keep in touch with her because they could always use a shifter on the inside.

Rayna had clung to that line, letting it give her hope as well as direct her appeal letter. She wrote back to the Academy, pleading with them to let her train there. Promising that she understood she'd never become a FUC field agent but also explaining that an education from FUC would be invaluable if she did decide to go into law enforcement on the human side while remaining a FUC contact.

To her extreme delight, she received a phone call not long after sending her appeal letter. Alyce Cooper, the FUCN'A director herself, informed her that her passion and determination had impressed and they were admitting her as a non-traditional cadet. Rayna accepted immediately.

It hadn't taken the other trainees long to notice Ray was different, especially since she didn't participate in any of the physical classes that required shifting. Instead, she was given research assignments and sent to the library.

And while the other cadets were nowhere near as cruel as the girls in her high school, it didn't escape Rayna's ears when they whispered the word. Mongrel.

RAYNA ENJOYED THE COMPANY OF THE BOOKS IN THE LIBRARY, especially in her favorite cozy spot. It was near the back, hidden between the stacks, where no one tended to venture.

Rayna was lucky. One of the librarians, Aubrey Taylor, had given birth recently, so she was happy to hand over plenty of research requests. Enough to keep Rayna busy—and earning research credits toward her cadet program.

When she was caught up with research requests, she still had plenty to occupy her time. While a lot of humans enjoyed listening to true crime podcasts, Rayna enjoyed reading about cold cases. It didn't surprise her to discover some of those unsolved crimes, serial killers never caught by humans, were rogue shifters with a taste for human flesh. Those cases remained unsolved for those left behind, but FUC files revealed the monsters had been brought to justice by their own kind.

Currently, though, she was reading about Miklos Bathory, a philosopher who'd documented the first cases of the supernatural world. His writings were now well sought after, and she felt fortunate to be in a place where she could peruse them.

Rayna glanced down at her watch. It was well past her designated library time. Her dorm mate, Suzanna, an overly excitable wolf shifter, had company and had asked Rayna to give her some time before coming back to the room. A pang of jealousy hit. Rayna didn't date. It was too hard to find anyone. She had no interest in dating humans, as she didn't want to be with someone who would never know the true nature of her parents... or why she could heal herself so quickly.

She was open to dating other shifters, but they weren't interested when they found out she couldn't shift. Rayna was more human than anything else in their eyes.

She pushed the thoughts of dating aside as she wondered if she should head out. It seemed she was completely alone. The library was never busy, since most of the students preferred the IT rooms over dusty old books, but there was usually at least one librarian around.

Rayna figured Aubrey wouldn't be here this late. The mouse shifter had explained to Rayna that ever since Merry had been born, she cut down on her working hours. Rayna couldn't blame her for wanting to spend time with her mate and their daughter.

Rayna tucked the file under her chin so she could use her hands to stand. It didn't matter if she possessed the healing ability and strength to rival most humans. Pins and needles still hit her with a speed that stole her breath. A quick look at her watch told her she'd been on the floor for a couple of hours. Rayna retrieved the folder and flopped forward, touching her toes. As the tips of her brunette hair brushed against the floor she caught sight of the white strands. She'd tried countless times to dye the section of her hair near her fringe, but it was resistant to hair dyes. Yet another marking her sign as different. The key around her neck dropped free from its hiding place down her top and fell into her line of sight.

She straightened and groaned as something clicked back into place, and then she wrapped a protective hand around the key. "I don't think Alyce would forgive me if I lost you."

Some of the Academy's more important files were now kept behind a locked door since the mysterious Miklos Bathory books had been the target of thieves on two separate occasions. Rayna walked over to the non-descript door and inserted the key. She typed a six-digit code into the keypad and waited for the red light to turn green. Then she counted to three, twisted the key, and heard a soft click. The door swung open as she turned the handle.

She safely stored the files and then re-locked the secure room before leaving the library. Rayna walked down the hallway and in the direction of the cafeteria. Her stomach had started rumbling, and she hoped there were still some of Maude's Meatless Meatballs left.

She didn't pass anyone else on her way. The place was quiet, the trainees either retired to their dorms to rest and study or headed out for the night. They lived near a town they affectionately called Nowheresville, and the only place of interest was a pub called the Hub—run by a shifter called Bear—but it was better than doing nothing.

The Academy offered many options for activities, all of the training variety. There was the gym, the pool, and the shooting range, but mostly the cadets chose to run around the woods in their animal forms. They were far enough away from civilization—with enough cloaking technology—none of them worried about being spotted by humans.

Nobody invited Rayna, and she wouldn't have gone even given the choice. Nothing reminded a person of their inability to shift more than to be surrounded by a bunch of shifters who could do the one thing she couldn't.

"I was about to come find you."

Rayna swiveled her head to see Alyce walking toward her. She instinctively took the key from around her neck and held it out to her. "I'd figured you were gone for the day. I was going to return it first thing tomorrow."

"I knew you would." Alyce glanced up and down the corridor. "Sweetheart, your grandmother has been trying to get ahold of you. She said she tried to call your mobile."

Ruth? Her parents were visiting her this weekend. Why would she be calling so late?

"I left my phone in the dorm. There wasn't any point taking it with me." The library didn't allow cell phones to be turned on. "Did she say what was wrong?"

"There was an accident. Your dad's been taken to the hospital."

"Is he okay?"

Alyce handed her cell phone to Rayna. "I really think you need to call your grandmother."

CHAPTER TWO

The world was a horrible place. Dark and unforgiving. Arimas—better known as Ari—Averus knew it better than most. The world could sap all the hope and joy out of the happiest person, leading them to struggle with finding meaning in such bleakness.

Ari would have given up on it all if it weren't for the one little spot of sunshine in his life. The tiniest little beacon of hope that kept him going each day. His daughter, Daisy.

She was why he came to work each day, even after he left FUC. Even after his precious wife, Becca, had died.

After Becca's death, it had taken him a while, but he had to do something to support Daisy. He couldn't go back to FUC. That organization was the cause of Becca's demise. If he hadn't been working for FUC, he wouldn't have gained enemies. People who wanted revenge for one reason or another. They wouldn't have targeted Becca.

No, he couldn't return to FUC, so he made something else of himself.

The Broker.

That was who he was now.

During his time as a FUC agent, he'd met plenty of shady people. Many of them he'd brought to justice, but those who remained free, he'd remembered. He used those connections now, offering his services as an information broker. His temporary office in British Columbia was small, located in an industrial estate far from the closest city. He didn't share the space with any neighbors, and like all of his meeting spaces, it was completely off the books. Nothing could be traced back to him. His public persona of Arimas Averus lived near the Lake District in the UK, in a village called Orchard. He traveled all over the world and ran a charity for human soldiers injured due to their time in service.

Ari did good things with his money. It wasn't all a lie.

And yet, he wasn't any closer to getting the thing he needed. Just one more thing he could blame on FUC.

A surge of anger swept through him, and a growl rumbled in his chest. His animal paced inside of him, restless. It had been a while since he had shifted, and it felt like his animal was trying to claw its way out. He took a couple of deep breaths, steadying his racing heart and regaining control. His office wasn't the ideal place for a seven-foot bear to let loose. His control had slipped the first time he hadn't gotten his hands on the book, and it had been a pain to get everything replaced.

"Sir, have you eaten yet?"

"Did you see me go out for food?" Ari snapped in annoyance at his assistant entering his office. For some reason, Kya continued to pester him, no matter how much he might try to push her away. At this point, she was the one constant in his life—besides Daisy, of course.

"You could have brought food on your way to the office," Kya replied, unperturbed.

He would have fired her out of spite if she wasn't so good at her job.

"I didn't," he practically growled at her.

"Then good thing I ordered your usual from the Oriental Chef. It'll be twenty minutes. Please don't chew on the furniture while you wait." She flashed him a smile and closed the door behind her.

Leave it to Kya. She'd said many times over the years that the one thing she prioritized over anything else was making sure the bear shifter remained fed.

Otherwise, Ari got *really* cranky.

The fox shifter never withered under Ari's cantankerous demeanor. Never left his side, even when he moved from office to office around the world. He thought that would have given her an excuse to find a new job—one with a boss who wasn't as bearish as he was—but she'd followed him everywhere. The picture of dedication.

It was because Kya knew what happened. What Ari had been through and why he did the things he did. *"You did what you needed to do for your cub,"* she'd said.

"If there was more time, I could have approached the situation differently. Paid for her help, instead of demanding it."

"I know."

He really wanted to wallow in his self-pity. Kya knew that and ignored his instructions to be left alone.

All he had wanted was the *Isten Teremtmenyei*. He could have found experts to decode the book or borrowed Aubrey Taylor for a couple of days. Jackson Holt had beaten Ari's mercenary, Layla, to the book. That had triggered the mess of events that had ended here, with Ari sitting in a sterile office, empty-handed.

Ari slumped forward in his chair, rubbing his forehead with the tips of his fingers. Daisy was the only reason he was still alive. After he lost Becca, something inside of him snapped.

Ari had loved his wife. They hadn't had a traditional

mating bond, and their animals had been wildly different—bear and rabbit, respectively. That hadn't made their love any less. Their human sides had been completely and utterly enamored with each other, and they had every reason to believe they'd have a happy-ever-after with each other. They knew it had worked out for others.

But they'd had no idea that there were rare cases when a mismatched shifter pair's offspring could suffer ill effects.

And now Daisy was dying because of their coupling. At least, that was what he'd been told. Doctor Stirling, a monkey shifter, had said Daisy had a month left, at the most. That felt like barely any time at all. Especially when there were no solutions to the problem. None publicly known, that was. If there was a cure, it might be held within the writings of Miklos Bathory.

But FUC wasn't letting a former-agent-turned-bad-guy like Ari get his hands on it.

Ari rubbed his face, glancing at the picture of Daisy on his desk. She slept a lot these days, and Hendrickson—another of Ari's assistants, who now served as nanny-housekeeper-cook—looked after her while Ari traveled. He hated leaving, knowing it might be the last time he would see her.

Ari crossed a thousand lines to keep his daughter safe, but it wasn't going to be enough. The book was his last hope, even though a long shot. He'd spent thousands of dollars, pounds, and yen on a multitude of different doctors, humans and shifters. How was it possible in a world filled with the impossible that he couldn't find a cure for her? The condition was tied to her genetic code, something that couldn't be fixed with modern medicine.

There was a soft knock on his office door, and he glanced up to see Kya. He hoped she'd come back with his lunch delivery, but her hands were empty. Normally, she worked hard to portray a light and cheerful mood, but her expression had grown serious.

"What is it, Kya?"

"You have a visitor, sir." Not Ari or Mr. Averus. It meant whatever she'd brought to him was business.

"I'm not really in the mood to take on new clients."

"I'm aware. This isn't a client though. I really think you should make time to talk to him. I'll bring in some coffee."

"And my lunch?"

"I haven't forgotten about it." Kya liked to push Ari's buttons, and she would do it with a smile on her face. He trusted her and gave her a brisk nod. The fox shifter opened the door further, and a man strolled into the office. He was tall, with a sharp pointy chin and thick black hair. There was an air of confidence about him, which Ari immediately disliked on principle. There was no doubt in his mind that the stranger was a shifter, though he couldn't place the animal. *Prey.*

He gestured to the chair opposite him.

"Thank you, Mr. Averus."

"You have me at a disadvantage." He hated to admit to something he considered a weakness. Ari made it his business to know everything about everyone. "What do I call you?"

"You can call me Mr. Black." He unbuttoned his dark navy suit jacket and sat.

Ari raised an eyebrow and studied him. If his name was really Mr. Black, then Ari dressed up like Lola Bunny on the weekends. No matter. Kya would have already entered the man's photo into the database, and it wouldn't take long for the system to spit out a real name, where he lived, his shoe size, and what he ate for breakfast.

"How can I help you, Mr. Black?" He had no real interest in taking any jobs. Daisy was his priority, and anything that took him away from her right now was not worth it.

"It's how I can help you. There's word on the streets that you're searching for something specific but haven't been able to obtain it yet."

Ari frowned. "And what is that?"

Instead of answering directly, the visitor took a different approach. "I know who you really are. I have managed to get my hands on some valuable information worth something to you."

It was a short list of people who knew who he truly was. The shifter in front of him wasn't on the list. "My name is Arimas Averus. It's not a secret." He moved his hand and rested it on the gun he kept under the desk.

The mysterious man chuckled. "We both know it's not as simple as that. Sure, it might be your public persona. but it's not who you truly are. You're the Broker." He raised his hands. "Before you shoot me, just listen to what I have to offer you. If you don't believe me, you can kill me. I won't even try to stop you."

"You're a shifter. A few bullets won't kill you if I don't hit anything vital."

"But they'll hurt, and it's something I'd rather not experience." Ari detected an accent Mr. Black seemed intent on hiding. Was he from England?

"You're a long way from home. Where are you from?"

"A place in Wales. You've never even heard of it. Not many people have."

That's a lie. Ari moved his hand from underneath the desk and rested both on top of it. It wasn't like he needed a weapon to kill the man in front of him. He let his bear come closer to the surface, knowing his eyes glowed golden. It was enough to send a clear message. Unless Mr. Black's creature was more dangerous than a bear—which he wasn't, based on the prey scent he exuded—the man wouldn't win in a fight. "What information are you selling?"

"It's valuable and wasn't easy to come by."

That wasn't a clear answer. "And how much do you want for this mysterious information?"

Mr. Black shrugged like he didn't know. Ari figured he wouldn't have come to the office if he didn't have an amount in mind. He was being coy. A trait Ari didn't appreciate.

Finally, Mr. Black said, "A million pounds."

Ari laughed. and the man frowned. Fuck coy, it took seriously big balls for anyone to come into his den asking for that kind of money. That was the only reason the visitor wasn't already dead.

"That's a lot of money, Mr. Black. How do I know if the information is worth the amount?"

"It's more than worth the amount. You've got my word."

"That means fuck all, Mr. Black. I think it's best if you tell me what you know, and I'll figure out if it's worth the amount you're asking for."

He glanced around, suddenly nervous. "I have people waiting for me. If I'm not out of here in ten minutes, I hope you're prepared for a fight."

There wasn't a bitter smell in the air that betrayed when someone was lying. Mr. Black actually had thought ahead.

"You have my word that I won't kill you," Ari promised.

"It's common knowledge in certain circles that your daughter is sick. I know about something that will heal her."

Another deep breath confirmed the man still wasn't lying. Hope built in the pit of Ari's stomach. He did his best to ignore it. He couldn't let such a dangerous emotion make decisions for him. He schooled his face into a picture of indifference. "Okay, you've got my attention. How?"

Mr. Black reached into the inside pocket of his suit jacket and pulled out a small sheet of paper. The shifter leaned forward and pushed the paper across to him. Ari glanced down and noted the numbers. "Those are my bank details. Send me the money first and I'll tell you."

"And if this is some kind of twisted scam?" Ari had dealt with plenty of people with loose morals. He hadn't survived for so long because he made stupid mistakes—the misstep with Lizzie Adams aside. Who could have known the thief he had hired would find her mate and turn on him?

"You can sense a lie, Mr. Averus. It's a well-known talent of yours. Why would I even try?"

For a hell of a lot of money and enough time to get out of the country. "Do I really need to state the obvious? I'll wire you half of the money now and the rest if your information pans out."

A thin layer of sweat gathered across Black's top lip. "And if it doesn't?"

A cruel smile crossed Ari's lips. "You know who I am, or at least you think you do. If I discover you have lied to me, you know there's nowhere you can hide, and I'm not a forgiving man."

CHAPTER THREE

Her dad was gone.

Rayna couldn't think past that one devastating sentence. She tried hard to focus on something, anything else but the cold hard truth kept creeping in.

There had been an accident. Her parents had been visiting her grandmother Ruth. Rayna's dad had dropped off her mum and headed out to pick up food from a restaurant, but the roads had been slippery. The police had said he'd taken the corner too fast, and the car had skidded off the road, the underside scraping against something—rocks or the trunk of a tree. The petrol tank had ruptured. Some passersby had seen the fire and called the police.

Her mum had slipped into a catatonic state. The shock of losing a mate was devastating to the one left behind. With her unique ability to heal others, her mum might have been able to save him, if she'd been with him. Rayna promised she would be on the next plane out. The Academy had the use of a private plane, and she'd been taken to the nearest international airport.

She put her headphones on and curled up in one of the

lounge chairs. It was the middle of the night, and the airport was mostly deserted. The next flight to London would leave in a couple of hours. The capital wasn't home, but she planned on renting a car and driving up to Redfield, a tiny village next to the Lake District. Ruth was still the alpha of one of the seal pods up there, and she informed Rayna that her mum would stay with her until she was better.

Ruth Jensen knew better than most the danger of losing a mate.

I can't believe he's really gone.

Her mum had been a little dubious about the idea of her only daughter enrolling in FUCN'A. Her dad, on the other hand, had pulled her into a tight hug. *"It's time you found your place in the world, kiddo. You're going to do brilliant things."*

The echo of his words brought tears to her eyes. She hadn't grieved yet. The wound was too fresh and unbelievable. She half expected her phone to burst into life and for him to tell her it had been a mistake, that he was okay. He was the only one, besides her mum, who believed in her, and she couldn't accept that he was gone. She wouldn't hear his voice anymore. Her chest went tight, and her vision blurred. It wasn't fair. Shifters weren't immortal, but they could heal a lot of damage. He should have walked away with a couple of bruises. If the car hadn't caught fire, he would have survived.

Why was he driving so fast?

There hadn't been time to process everything, just a few frantic hours between a phone call with her grandmother and packing up her things. Everything crashed down on her. She'd been going since classes had started at seven that morning, and after, she'd gone to the library. She was exhausted.

The first time she arrived in Canada, the airport had been a hive of activity. Tourists. People returning from their holidays. She'd been swept up in all of the excitement.

Besides her life in the UK and the one ill-advised trip to China, she'd never left the country. She'd walked around with eyes wide and with a look of disbelief on her face. Even the language had been different. A mixture of English and French. The entire world had opened up for her in a way she had never experienced before. Even if she knew her time at the Academy wouldn't be easy, the challenge hadn't scared her. Now she was terrified about what waited for her at home.

"I'll take a whisky, no ice."

Suddenly it wasn't just Rayna and the bored bartender. A man had entered the lounge and headed for the bar. Out of curiosity and boredom and the need for any kind of distraction, Rayna switched off her headphones.

"Would you prefer the eighteen or twenty-one?"

"The twenty-one." The stranger shrugged his jacket off and placed it on the back of the chair next to him. Rayna watched as he rolled up his sleeves, and she caught sight of a tattoo.

The bartender gave a brisk nod and got to work. Rayna half-expected him to just pour the whisky into a glass. Instead, he studied the glass, making sure it was clean, deemed it unworthy, and selected another. After he gave it the same scrutiny, he poured out a healthy measure. When he was finished, he presented the glass to the man. *Damn, he's really hoping for a tip.* He hadn't been that bothered when he'd given her the bottle of water. Who accepted the drink with a nod of thanks.

"Thanks, it's been a long day."

"We don't get many guests this late. Where are you off to?"

"I'm heading to the UK. Lake District. My plane is being refueled, and I thought I'd walk the terminal to stretch my legs before the long flight." He took a sip from his glass and sighed in pleasure. "I hate traveling in the middle of the night, but at least there aren't any crowds to worry about."

Who the hell is this guy, traveling by private plane? Is he an actor or a businessman? There was an air of confidence about him.

"This is a slow shift at the best of times," the bartender agreed. Then he looked across at Rayna and noticed she was watching them. He smiled. "Looks like you're not the only one traveling at stupid o'clock at night."

But I'm not traveling by private plane. Her cheeks burned under the unexpected scrutiny. She didn't bother to remove her headphones. Rayna didn't really want to talk to anyone, even if a moment ago a distraction was all she wanted. The man turned his seat and smiled at her. The word handsome didn't do him justice. His dark wavy hair matched his eyes, and Rayna blushed every harder.

"Can I get you a drink?"

She shook her head. Then gestured to her headphones, letting them think she was still listening to something. The man frowned, but Rayna picked up a paperback that had been left on the table, flicking it open. The message should have been clear, She didn't want to talk. After a moment, she sensed someone standing next to her. She glanced up in surprise and met the dark gaze of the stranger. Rayna frowned, raising the book slightly to say, *Leave me alone.*

"It's upside down."

For a second his words didn't register, and then Rayna looked at the book. *Damn, he's right.* Her face grew warm again. She rested the book on her knees and finally took her headphones off. "I didn't even notice."

The corner of his lip twitched. "Also, you haven't been listening to music since I walked in here."

"How do you know that?" Then it clicked. Rayna had met plenty of confident people during her time at the Academy.

They were the kinds of people who could walk into a room, pick someone, and get all the information they needed out of them. "You're a shifter."

He nodded. "Can I sit?"

She gestured at the available chair with a shrug. Tall, Dark, and Unbelievably Handsome sat opposite her. He draped his jacket across his knees.

"I'm Arimas. But my friends call me Ari."

"Rayna."

"You're from the Academy, aren't you?"

"How do you know that?" Her hackles rose. She remembered the security breaches that had happened over the last six months since she'd been a cadet. People wanted information on FUC and information on the Academy. FUC had enemies, and it wasn't out of the scope of reality that this man—Ari—was trying to get information out of her.

Rayna rubbed the bridge of her nose. It was more than likely. She'd need to tread carefully.

"Lucky guess," he replied. "This is the only international airport close enough to the Academy, you recognized me as a shifter, and you have that certain soon-to-be-agent air about you."

"You looked at me and thought trainee." She didn't correct his incorrect assumption that she'd become an agent someday.

"It seemed to track, judging by your age, though I wouldn't rule out entry-level staff," he said with a smile before taking a sip of his drink.

"Have you attended the Academy?" she asked, not confirming or denying his assessment.

"No, the Academy came along well after I'd become an agent."

She raised an eyebrow. If he was an agent, it would mean

she could speak more freely in front of him. But what were the odds that he was lying? "You're in FUC?"

"I'm not anymore." A shadow crossed his face, and she decided to avoid digging any further.

"What do you do now?"

"I work for various nonprofits. I'm here in BC looking at a veterans hospital that sent out an invite for me to visit."

Figuring out if someone was lying wasn't one of the abilities Rayna had. Only some shifters could naturally sniff out lies. Others could develop it, but unfortunately, it seemed like Rayna never would. That was why she trained twice as hard on reading people without the shifter assist.

"What are you flying out for?" he asked, bumping her out of her attempts at lie detection.

"I'm visiting family," she told him, keeping it vague. She wasn't sure she could get the words out, let alone deal with sympathy from a random stranger if she shared that she was heading to her father's funeral. "My grandmother lives in Redfield."

"I live in Orchard."

There were three small villages around the Lake District, specifically for shifters. Rayna knew the people who lived in Orchard had a ridiculous amount of money. She supposed that was how he afforded his private plane.

Just then, his phone pinged with a text. He checked it and then looked back at Rayna. "The next commercial flight to London isn't for hours, and I'm about to leave now. There's plenty of room for another passenger if you'd like to join me."

His suggestion took her completely by surprise. It wasn't a clever idea to catch a lift with a stranger, even if they were both shifters. That was the start of a lot of horror stories.

"I really do want to get there quickly," she mumbled to herself.

"I'll be landing close to the Lake District, too. Which means you can cut six hours of traveling by car from London to Redfield," he offered.

"Serial killer?"

"Excuse me?" he sputtered in surprise.

"Are you one? It's a legitimate question."

"True, but if I was, would I admit to being one?"

She took a sip of her water. She tended to trust her gut, especially after honing it at the Academy—intuition classes had been one of the ones she'd excelled at. It wasn't infallible though. "Okay, I'll accept your generous offer. On one condition though."

"You don't trust easily, do you?"

"Not as a general rule."

He frowned then shrugged. "What's the condition?"

"I take your photo and send it to my grandmother." It was possible Ruth knew who he was. She had a network of people who were in her pod.

He smiled, and she fought against the urge to fan herself. "Not a problem." He leaned back in the oversized red leather chair, his arms opened wide, legs crossed at the ankles. The picture of ease.

She snapped a photo and started to write out a quick message to Ruth. "Where's your airstrip?" If her grandmother couldn't vouch for him, she'd send it to Alyce. Ari might have said he was an agent before the Academy existed, but that didn't mean someone wouldn't be able to recognize him.

CHAPTER FOUR

While the excuse to stretch his legs was valid, it really wasn't the reason Ari had ventured into the terminal that night.

He was there to meet the woman Mr. Black promised was the key to healing Daisy.

Rayna Jensen was a caladrius, from the powerful Aikawa family, who were known for their ability to heal others. Their gift was so unique that Ari had never heard even a whisper of their existence.

Which meant they'd been keeping their gift a secret. Ari couldn't just walk up to her and ask her to heal Daisy. And besides that, Rayna might not even know she had the ability. In the information he'd managed to gather, he'd learned that she could heal herself, but there was no record of her healing others.

Mr. Black suggested that was tied to her inability to shift. Unlock that and unlock her healing powers as well. She just needed the right push...

There were two ways he could play the encounter with

Rayna Jensen. His first instinct had been to kidnap and keep her hostage until she healed his daughter.

Mr. Black had told him it wouldn't be an option. Ari needed to gain her trust because the caladrius only bestowed their gift if they wanted to—not if forced.

That meant lying to her.

His intel on her revealed that she didn't have the ability to detect lies, which played in his favor. Even so, he decided to keep his words as truthful as possible with small talk.

It was a challenge to project a cool composure. Ari didn't like being in the field. It raised a lot of issues, and while nobody knew what the Broker looked like, people knew who Arimas Averus was. Especially here.

He'd been lucky that she had decided to catch the red eye. The mostly empty airport meant his visit so close to the Academy wouldn't be noted by anyone. He had no intention of creating ripples. Not when he was so close to a cure for Daisy.

If anyone found out who he truly was now, everything would be lost. In his role as the Broker, he had pissed off a lot of people who had once been friends. It hadn't been personal, and he had made sure that, for all intents and purposes, Arimas Averus had cut all ties with his former organization.

She finished sending his photo to her grandmother and pocketed her phone. "All right, let's go."

She started to gather her small roller bag, and he took the handle from her. "Allow me."

He watched as she blushed again, her darkened cheeks making her look even more beautiful. He had tried not to focus on her appearance as he'd spied her in the lounge. The dark brunette hair with the white steak at the front was pulled back into a messy bun. Those dark haunted eyes, easy to read and filled with pain. Rayna was fragile and hurting on a deep emotional level. Ari understood the pain she felt.

One he had experienced himself. As she blinked, tears rolled down her cheeks, and she wiped them away.

"Are you okay?"

She nodded. "Lead the way."

Ari wasn't a fan of flying, but when you traveled all over the world, it really was the only way to get about. He had a particular company he hired, and they offered him privacy, transporting him from one side of the planet to the other. Rayna's eyes had widened slightly as she spied the plane. Impressed.

She followed him onboard. "You travel this way a lot?"

"Every couple of months. You like it?"

"It's above my pay grade." She slumped into one of the chairs, stretching out her legs before curling up in the chair.

"It suits you." Ari put his laptop case into a compartment. He wasn't going to be able to work with her close. Rayna wasn't easy to read. The emotional pain was there, and it masked everything else.

"The plane?" she asked, bemused.

He smiled and approached the minibar. "Do you want a drink?" The well-stocked fridge was filled with a variety of beverages, alcoholic and non. "There's a large selection."

"A bottle of water."

Ari had worked out which airport Rayna would go to. It wasn't difficult. It was the one nearest to the Academy. It also hadn't taken Ari long to figure out who Rayna Jensen was, her history and family. It was an open book to anyone with their fingers in the dark, shadowy world of the black market. He'd also made the point to check social media; Rayna wasn't on any of them.

He liked that.

She was shy and a tired and an emotional wreck. Her skin was pale, and she had dark circles under her eyes. She seemed comfortable curled up in that chair, trapped in her own dark thoughts. Her father was gone. A tragic accident for sure but one Ari could take advantage of.

Though he couldn't help but wonder what role the mysterious Mr. Black had played in the sudden death of Adam Jensen. He hoped none, that this was all just a coincidence, but even if it wasn't, he had to keep his focus on what was important here. Saving Daisy.

He handed her the water bottle and put his in the little dip in the table, kept in place by the quirk of design. He glanced out of the window. It was dark outside. Tiny beads of light moved around the tarmac as the pilot went through his final checks. Ari always felt a bit of nerves before takeoff. His bear wasn't a fan of flying. He preferred to keep their paws on the ground.

The pilot's voice came on the intercom to go through the safety spiel, and Ari stretched out, placing his feet underneath Rayna's chair. With a sigh, he closed his eyes. The flight to Toronto would only take a couple of hours. There they'd refuel before the transatlantic portion of the trip.

At least the hard part was over. He had made contact with his target and had her in his custody. A part of him wanted to continue talking to Rayna. It was nice to have someone respond to his charming act. Back when he'd been a field agent, there hadn't been many people immune to it. Of course, that was before he married Becca.

He tried not to think about her. It was a path that only led down a world of regret. The life before he had become the Broker. When he had been creating enemies for himself. People who broke the rules without any thought of the consequences because they thought they were above the law. It had been the actions of one that had changed the course of

Ari's life. Daisy would still be facing an early death, but Becca would still be here, and he wouldn't have to face it alone.

Bang.

Ari flinched. He opened his eyes to see the flight attendant closing a cabinet. He glared at the man, who must have felt the weight of his stare because he glanced in Ari's direction, and all the color drained from his face. The younger man muttered an apology and scurried off to finish his list of tasks. Suddenly Rayna's head appeared from over her chair.

"Are you okay?"

"I'm fine," he said, taking a page out of her book. She hadn't told him why she was upset, and Ari saw no reason to divulge any of his own past. He needed to gain her trust. The surest way was to seduce her, but she definitely wasn't in the mood for that. Also, he wasn't crass enough to hit on a grieving woman. He'd need another way in. He had until the plane touched asphalt at the airport to get her number.

She frowned. "You sure?"

"Why do you ask?"

Rayna shook her head slightly. "I don't know. I'm sorry. You don't need to tell me anything. We don't know each other."

He crossed his arms, studying her. It was enjoyable watching the cogs in her brain tick over. "That's true. We've got some time to get to know each other though. Interested?"

She bit her lip, clearly unsure, though he thought she seemed to need a friend right now.

He smiled. "No pressure, but if you want to take a peek inside my mind, it's only fair if I get to have a peek in yours."

Her cheeks went a wonderful shade of pink. Ari hadn't been sure what to expect from her. Rayna came from money, and women like that usually had a bucketful of confidence. They knew how to dress, how to move, and how to speak.

Any of that might have been hidden by the grief she was

going through, but he was a savvy enough former agent to see that the way she presented herself now wouldn't be too far from her usual dress. Casual. No designer shoes or bags.

He also had to factor in the fractured relationship with her mum's family and the fact that she couldn't shift. Both of those were strong enough reasons for her to lack confidence in a world of shifters. She hadn't let that define her. It was impressive.

Besides, he couldn't feel sorry for her. He knew what he needed to do. A random woman didn't compare to Daisy. Ari would burn the world to the ground to save his daughter.

"Okay, I'm a little too wired to sleep anyway."

Ari patted the empty chair next to him. "So, you don't have to twist around to talk to me."

She nodded, quickly got to her feet, and joined him. The plane would be taking off soon. Being so close to her made the hair stand up on the back of his neck. Even his bear stirred as she sat down, which was odd. Ari had kept a clear line between him and others since Becca's death. Even when he shifted, he was by himself. Now his bear cried out, desperate for the company of their own kind.

She can't shift, he reminded his bear.

For now.

CHAPTER FIVE

RAYNA DIDN'T KNOW THE PRECISE MOMENT SHE FELL ASLEEP. One minute she had been talking to Ari and the next, she was waking up, her head resting on his shoulder. For a second, she went completely rigid. Judging from the soft rise and fall of Ari's chest, he was still asleep.

There was something incredibly comforting about using him like a pillow. She took a deep breath, trying to calm her racing heart. He had pulled the blind down, but the light shone through the cracks. There wasn't much time left before they arrived and she had to face all the pain that waited for her.

She hadn't found out much about the man she rested on. He had a knack for turning the focus of the conversation back to her. Either way, she felt oddly at peace, and she hadn't felt that way for a long time. What was it about him?

She reluctantly pulled away from him. Ari had moved his chair back to make himself more comfortable, and she glanced down at him. His dark eyelashes created half-moons against the tops of his cheeks. A full bottom lip. His black hair had been brushed away from his face, but strands now rested against his forehead.

"If you keep staring at me, you're going to give me a complex."

Rayna noticed she had moved back toward him, tempted to close her eyes again, but he was watching her. Her face burned hot, and she turned away. "I wasn't staring."

He stretched out next to her, his arms above his head, and then he relaxed. "Really?"

She turned back to face him, noting the way his shirt had come free of the waistband of his navy trousers. "It's not fair."

He frowned. "What do you mean?"

"How can you look that good after sleeping in a chair? I bet I look like I've been dragged through a hedge backward." She pulled the hair tie free and ran her fingers through her hair. Then she started to retie the heavy strands out of the way again.

"You think I look good?"

She peered down at him. He hadn't moved from his seat, but he appeared more relaxed than anyone should be after so many hours on a plane. "You own a mirror, right? You know you look good." There was a sharp snap of pain against her wrist as the hair tie broke. "Damn it." Rayna dropped the useless hair tie into her lap. "That's the third one this week. I didn't even think to pack my hairbrush."

He sat up next to her. "Let me." She flinched as he reached out to her. "Trust me, Rayna. This isn't the first time I've dealt with unruly hair. I've even got a spare hair tie."

"Odd thing for a man to carry." She turned around and held herself perfectly still as he ran his fingers through her hair. The urge to shiver nearly overtook her, but she managed to stop herself. *Oh goodness, why does that feel so good?* The way he worked out every knot proved he hadn't been lying when he said he had experience.

Rayna closed her eyes and let herself relax.

"You like that?"

"Yes." The word was drawn out and sounded like a moan. She jerked away from him. "I mean…"

He chuckled. "You don't need to explain. I have to do this sort of thing for Daisy, that's why I have a spare."

She stiffened. "Who's Daisy?"

"My daughter."

"You're married?" If there was a daughter, there was likely a wife, though Rayna hadn't noticed a wedding band on his finger.

He moved from brushing her hair with his fingers to handling the heavy strands with practiced ease. Then a twist and her stomach flipped as her hair was pulled taut.

"I was. It was a long time ago."

Suddenly his voice was next to her ear, his breathing hot against her skin. Rayna shivered. She hadn't wanted to fall to his charms, but Ari's voice did amazing things to her. Rayna turned and caught sight of the flecks of gold in his eyes.

For a long moment, they watched each other.

"Greetings, folks. We'll be landing at the strip within the hour."

The pilot could have told them the plane was taking a nosedive into the Thames and Rayna wouldn't have cared. The corner of Ari's lips curled into a smile, the look in his dark gaze full of promise. Everything about this situation was insane, but she couldn't deny her body's reaction to him. She trusted him, which made no sense since she didn't even know him.

"Your hair is done."

He was still too close, but Rayna didn't want to move away from him. "Thanks."

Ari eased himself back into his seat. "Do you have any free time while you visit family?"

"I don't think so. I've got to help my nan with preparations."

"Preparations?" He frowned, looking visibly confused.

"My dad's funeral." She hadn't told him that part yet. Hadn't said those words out loud at all. Now they caught in her mouth, and she felt her eyes start to burn. "Crap, I really didn't want to cry."

The elation of being close to him and the effect he had on her vanished.

"What happened?"

"A car accident."

"I'm sorry."

"It's okay. It's not like you had anything to do with it. He took a corner too fast, and he crashed." She took a deep breath, trying like hell not to cry. Why was she telling him all this? It didn't have anything to do with him and here she was spilling her guts to Tall, Dark, and Stupidly Attractive. If there was a swifter way to end something before it had truly begun, mentioning death was a good one.

"When was the last time you saw him?"

"A couple of months before I went to join the Academy." Suddenly there was a pressure on her hand, and she glanced down to see his resting on top of hers.

"He must have been really proud of you."

Rayna nodded. "They both were." She didn't raise her head to make eye contact with him. She suspected that would be her undoing.

They sat like that for a while. His animal must have sensed the distress she was in because something swept over her. A warmth that traveled all the way down her toes. Was this what it was like with other shifters? Rayna had always missed out on moments like this. The shifters she had known hadn't been interested in getting close to a mongrel. She never craved the closeness, because what would have been the point?

"If you get time, you should come and visit me before you return to the Academy."

His words took her by surprise. "Why?"

"Because I'm not the only one who feels this connection, am I?"

"I really don't have time." Didn't he know that she was broken? That had to be the only reason why he invited her because he didn't know she didn't have an animal.

Besides, there were a lot of things to plan, and she doubted her mum would be in a fit state to make any of those decisions herself. Her grandmother could handle a lot of it—as the head of her pod, she had experience with funerals—but the situation would likely hit differently, being it was for her son. Rayna's mum would need her support, too. Shifters who lost their mates had a terrible time adjusting to a world without them.

Rayna found herself glancing up, and as their eyes met, there was a jolt again. The closest thing to describe it was a static shock.

He broke eye contact. "Okay, how about we swap numbers? I really would like to meet you again. I could show you around the area and take you out to dinner. I know that sounds strange, considering the situation, but trust me. I know grief, and I also know it will do you some good to take a break from the heaviness of it all and breathe for yourself for an hour or two."

"I'm not going to make for the best of company."

"Let me worry about that. You strike me as someone who thinks of everyone before they think of themselves. When you need an escape, Rayna—and believe me you will—you can call me. I'll be there."

"Are you sure? I don't want to impose."

Ari smiled, and she found herself smiling back. "I wouldn't have offered if I believed you'd be imposing on me. I work a lot, and I can't remember the last time I had dinner with anyone besides my daughter, and I rarely get the chance to talk about something else besides work or children's cartoons. You'll be doing me a favor."

CHAPTER SIX

HE WATCHED AS RAYNA WALKED TO THE WOMAN WAITING BY the car.

The flight had been informative, if a little confusing. He thought he pulled out some of his best moves but, other than a twinge of interest, nothing. It had taken her hours to even admit her dad had died.

Clearly, his skills were rusty.

He hadn't been able to secure a second meeting, but at least he'd gotten her number. Even so, he couldn't call right away. Couldn't chase after her or seem in any way too eager. Everything hung on a razor-thin edge. If he came on too strong, she would pull away and his chance would be gone. Rayna would need to come to him.

He pretended to do something with his suitcase and made his way to the rental car, observing Rayna and the woman he assumed was her grandmother. Ruth Jensen, seal shifter. She had short grey hair and pale blue eyes. There was no telling how old she truly was. To a human, she might have looked in her early forties but shifters aged at a slower rate than humans. She was dressed in jeans, boots, and an oversized grey woolen jumper. Rayna ran toward her, and the woman pulled her into a fierce hug.

His phone burst to life in his pocket, and he pulled it free.

"Hello?" He turned away from the embracing pair, even as he caught the sounds of crying. His bear paced inside of him, not liking the sound of Rayna in distress. He wanted to go to her, comfort her. Ari shook his head.

"Sir, I still haven't been able to find information about the mysterious Mr. Black." Kya's voice held a twinge of anxiety. Not something he heard often. Understandable, given how odd the situation was.

"What about *her*?"

"A little. I sent the file to Hendrickson."

"Thank you, Kya. When will you arrive?" Traveling separately had been the best way to ensure he had plenty of opportunity to get close to Rayna.

"In a couple of days. I'm going to dig a little deeper into Mr. Black's real identity. I'll keep you updated."

"Be careful, Kya."

The fox shifter chuckled. "Careful, boss. You almost sound concerned about my safety."

"I'm being serious. He went to a lot of trouble to keep his identity a secret." Ari didn't like unanswered questions. The whole situation was off. If he had more time, he would have known everything before he even approached Rayna. Working this way wasn't wise, but he wasn't about to let a perfect opportunity slip past him.

"I'll be fine."

Ari didn't live in an oversized mansion. Nothing would draw the attention of unwanted eyes faster than a home that screamed "evil lair." Even so, he did live in an area known for its wealthy citizens, so he couldn't call his estate small by any means.

When he reached his home, he pulled up to the gate and typed in the code. He also gave the camera a brisk wave. If Kya had managed to get a hold of Hendrickson, he'd be waiting by the front door. And he wouldn't be alone. The gates swung open, and he made his way up the driveway. He'd barely parked and left his car when the front doors of the house opened.

"Daddy!"

He smiled broadly as he caught sight of his daughter in Hendrickson's arms. Usually, she ran down the steps and jumped into his awaiting bear hug. He noted her pale skin and the bruises underneath her eyes. A pang of sadness hit him, but he pushed the feeling aside, and he went to join them on the steps.

"Hello, beautiful. I brought you something." He reached into the front of his suitcase, a pocket that usually only fit a laptop but bulged with his gift, and pulled free a teddy bear.

"I missed you." Daisy reached for him, and his friend let her go. Daisy climbed into Ari's arms.

"I missed you too." She practically weighed little more than air. His bear growled in frustration. He could smell the sickness. Rayna didn't have the ability to shift but suffered no real ill effects. What was the difference between the pair? Why was his daughter dying but Rayna had survived into adulthood? He wriggled the teddy bear in front of her. "What should we name him?"

The little girl frowned like she was thinking about the world's most difficult puzzle. Then she smiled, and the tightness in Ari's chest eased. *Hold on for a little longer. I'm going to fix this. I promise.* "Daddy."

"But that's my name."

"He's an extra soft teddy bear, like you."

He brushed a kiss across her forehead. "Let's get you back to bed."

"I'm not tired," Daisy yawned. He readjusted her in his arms, the teddy bear squished between them as she rested her head on his shoulder.

"I know."

Hendrickson watched him with a guarded expression on his face. There was something on his mind, but he knew better than to bring up work in front of Daisy. Ari wanted her to have a normal life in the short amount of time she had left. There was no point in saying things around her that would confuse her. She knew her dad ran a charity, and he was a shifter, but she had never asked why she couldn't do the same. Cubs had the ability to shift young or when puberty hit.

"Is everything okay?" Ari asked as he walked into the house and toward Daisy's room.

His friend shook his head.

"Everything's fine." The gesture conflicted with his words. "I wanted to talk to you about dinner. Should we order in for a change?" Hendrickson was a brilliant cook, much better than Ari, having learned from his travels around the world.

"Good idea."

Ari nudged Daisy's door open with his foot. She was asleep in his arms but stirred slightly. Hendrickson moved in front of him, pulling the colorful screens aside and letting him reach the hospital bed without issue. With the utmost care, he laid her down on the bed and reattached the strap to her arm. The beeps quickened, and her eyes fluttered open. "Where are you going, Daddy?"

"I'll see you in a minute, beautiful. You want Chinese?"

"I'm not hungry."

He brushed a kiss against her clammy skin. "I know, but you need to eat to keep your strength up."

"Okay, Daddy. I'll try."

It broke his heart to see her like this, knowing it was his fault. "Get some rest. I need to talk to Henny."

She curled up on her side, closing her eyes, and Ari left with Hendrickson. He closed the door behind him. "How is she?"

"Not well. She spent a lot more time asleep than awake while you were away."

"We knew that would happen." He rubbed the bridge of his nose. "Why does it look like someone ran over your dog?"

He walked down the hallway and to his office. Everything was dark, and he opened the curtains, letting in the remaining evening light. Besides the temporary base in Canada, he spent most of his time in this office. There were several bookshelves against the right wall containing not just research tomes but also framed photos of Becca and a younger Daisy and a small selection of picture books that Daisy liked to look at when she was in his office. Against the opposite wall, there was a dark leather futon. It wasn't the most comfortable thing to sit on but was the perfect size for Daisy.

"A few warning bells were triggered," Hendrickson finally explained.

Ari frowned. "Warning bells" was the term they used to describe someone searching for information about him. Not Ari but the Broker.

"What does that matter? There's nothing tying the Broker to me. We've always been incredibly careful about that."

"I don't like it. You've been messing with FUC plans recently. You don't want to be on their shit list. Not now, not ever."

Ari pulled his chair out and sat down, stretched his legs out, and rested his head against the leather headrest. "I can't help Daisy without stepping on a few toes."

"And that was fine when nobody knew who you were, but now you've come out of the shadows. You're in contact with a trainee."

Ari didn't even bother to open his eyes. He hated traveling by planes, and he'd been in a state of hyper-awareness when Rayna slept next to him. His bear had been intrigued by her, and even Ari felt something he wasn't willing to admit to himself. It had distracted enough that he'd failed to rest, and he really needed to catch up on it now. "I need to get some sleep. Order our usual and wake me up when it gets here."

"What happens if she figures out who you really are? If she is smart, it won't take her long."

"Then I'll have to kill her."

CHAPTER SEVEN

Rayna had mostly been able to hold it together for the entire trip back to the UK. Then her grandmother hugged her, and the dam broke like tissue paper.

While her relationship with her mum's parents wasn't great, her father's mum—*please call me Ruth*—was a different story. She had always accepted Rayna without question and had never made her feel anything less than a welcome addition to the family.

Ruth ushered Rayna into the back seat of the car with her. Rayna didn't recognize the driver. The pretty woman with short-cropped hair was probably a member of her grandmother's pod.

They started off in the opposite direction of Orchard. She still felt Ari's fingers in her hair, styling the strands with an ease that took her breath away. There had been something about him that called to her on a primal level. A normal person would have questioned it, but Rayna didn't have the opportunity to even entertain it. Not when she had such heaviness ahead of her.

"How's she doing?"

"Her heart has been broken. She hasn't spoken since she found out what happened to Adam."

Rayna glanced out of the window, watching the pretty landscape full of lush green trees and hills rush past. On the left were the lakes, and the setting sun made the water sparkle. When the funeral ritual started, the lakes would hide her father's body deep beneath their surface. "I still can't believe this."

"That stretch of road has always been dangerous." Her voice was filled with the sadness of a mother grieving her son.

"Why would he be driving that fast? He isn't—" The word caught in her throat. "He wasn't like that."

"I don't know much more than you." Her grandmother tapped her fingers against the door, deep in thought. "Your dad went to collect dinner. It was a fifteen-minute drive down the road. He's done the trip a hundred times before without incident. I don't know what happened." There was a rumbling sound deep within her grandmother's chest. A mixture of grief, anger, and frustration.

"Are they investigating further or just writing it off as an accident?"

"They think it was an accident, but I have my people investigating. It's not that I don't trust the police, but they won't be looking for the same signs as our kind will."

"Do *you* think it was an accident?" The question had been playing on Rayna's mind since she found out what happened. She couldn't get her head around the idea he might have been speeding.

"Everybody loved your father."

That wasn't precisely true, but Rayna didn't question it. Her grandmother knew the truth, that Rayna's grandparents on her mother's side had never liked her father. They blamed him for muddling the gene pool, fathering a mongrel who hadn't inherited the caladrius. Would they kill him because of it? Rayna was twenty-one now. That was a long time to wait for revenge.

She wiped a few stray tears away. "But you think it's at least a possibility?"

"It's nothing you need to worry about. You need to focus on your mum. She needs you. How long do you have before you need to return to the Academy?"

"A few weeks. The director said to take off as much time as I needed, but I don't want to push my luck."

The car stopped at a set of traffic lights. There were many similarities between certain parts of Canada and the Lake District. They were both beautiful and peaceful. The Lake District was a popular tourist location for its stunning views and history, but since it was the off-season, it wasn't as busy as it normally was. There were still a handful of tourists, but they tended to stay in the human villages. Poppyfield, Redfield, and Orchard were primarily for shifters. There weren't any hotels or inns, but that didn't stop the occasional humans from walking around the villages.

"You know you don't have to go back there, don't you? If you wanted to stay here and attend a local university, I could pay the tuition for you."

Her grandmother's voice pulled Rayna away from her thoughts. "I want to be there."

She sighed. "You have a place here, with the pod."

Rayna glanced across at her grandmother. Ruth Jensen had always been full of almost endless energy. She wore an easy smile on her face even with all the responsibilities that weighed heavily on her shoulders. Even after her mate had passed years ago, she'd still managed to seem full of life. But now, with the death of her son, she appeared almost deflated, tired.

"I know, but that's not what I want."

"I know," she replied with a sad smile. "I just can't bear to lose someone else."

Rayna was thankful her grandmother didn't want to argue with her. It wasn't the time or place. "Can you keep me updated about what your people find?"

"Of course."

<hr>

RAYNA DROPPED HER SUITCASE IN THE HALLWAY. HER DAD smiled down at her from photos on the wall. The sight was like an emotional gut punch, and she looked down at the floor. She wanted to be strong, but those familiar eyes, the soft creases around them as if the photographer caught him mid-laugh, battered at her defenses.

"She hasn't left the guest room in the attic. I was going to take up some sweet tea, but she might actually drink it if it comes from you."

"I'll do that."

She headed down the hallway and into the brightly lit kitchen. The first thing she noticed was the smell—a combination of honeysuckle, vanilla, and lavender. The next thing she noticed was the man in front of the kettle.

"Uncle Declan."

He turned, opening his arms for Rayna to launch herself at him. "Hello, love."

She pulled away from him and assessed the man in front of her. He'd always reminded her of her father, there was a distinct resemblance between the pair that was difficult to ignore. The same height, broad shoulders, and eye color. Where her father took his responsibilities as eldest seriously, Declan never had to worry about any of that. His life hadn't been planned out for him. For the most part, he'd been left to his own devices and with that freedom, he traveled around the world. It almost made him the black sheep of the family. Pods were close-knit, a sense of community was important to them, and they rarely left the town. Declan had always craved his freedom and took every opportunity that came his way.

"I thought you were still traveling.'

"I arrived last night. It's good to see you. I wish it was under better circumstances." He picked up one of the cups and handed it to her. "I've been trying to get her to drink something, but she isn't interested. I don't think she knows when I'm in the room with her."

She glanced at her grandmother, who'd followed her into the kitchen. "Is that normal?"

"It can be, but we need to break through to her sooner, rather than later."

What could anyone say that would make Hiriko feel better? She had lost her mate, her other half. The world was never going to be the same again. "Tell me what I can do to help."

"Let her know she isn't alone. That there are things still worth living for. It won't be easy, but we can't let her vanish into the darkness, or we risk losing her completely."

Rayna took the cup.

"I better go and see her." Both of them looked at her with worry in their eyes, but her grandmother gave her a solemn nod.

Rayna's chest grew tight as she walked up the stairs. She kept her gaze straight, not looking at the photos that lined the walls. As she turned a corner, facing the last set of stairs that led up to the attic, she stopped.

Wedding photos. Others from when Rayna was a baby, held in her dad's arm as he smiled down at her. The grandpa she never met dressed in a smart suit with a twinkle in his eye. Why had her grandmother chosen to line them up there, out of sight? Near the top was one final photograph. Her heart twisted painfully at the sight of the three of them together. Bright smiles. Her mum had never looked more beautiful, nor her dad more handsome. Rayna was all chubby cheeks with her telltale streak of white hair in between her dark strands.

She smiled, but she couldn't shake the immense sense of sadness. Someone had taken her dad away from her. A man with a kind heart and the willingness to help anyone who asked for it. Hell, sometimes he didn't even have to be asked. He just knew.

Now he's gone.

She tried to bring her breathing back under control before she continued up the stairs, knocking softly on the door. Without waiting for a reply, she entered.

There was a rhythmic sound of wood creaking. Like all of the rooms in her grandmother's house, it was kept in good condition, dust-free with no musty smell. Rayna didn't know who had moved the rocking chair, her mum or grandmother, but it had ended up in the alcove by the window, which gave a clear view of the horizon, houses as far as the eye could see. A woman sat in the chair, a tartan shawl wrapped around her shoulders. Her hair was a vibrant white, which held a warmth that even a professional hairdresser would find difficult to reproduce and maintain. The woman barely acknowledged Rayna as she placed the cup on the table and knelt beside her.

"Hi, Mum."

At the sound of her voice, her mum turned her head. Rayna had never seen her so lost before. "Rayna?"

CHAPTER EIGHT

Ari knew why she hadn't called. Even a traditional human funeral service would have someone tied up in the procedures and traditions.

Adam Jensen hadn't been human though. A member of a seal pod, his body would be taken to the depths of the lake and buried in one of the hidden caves. The body had been collected from the human morgue by Ruth's people at the beginning of the week.

The death of the eldest son of Jensen pod had been big news, sending ripples through the shifter world. It wasn't difficult to find information. Now the ritual was over, and Rayna would return to the Academy.

Did I read the situation wrong? Maybe she didn't feel the same irrational spark as I did?

Ari had entertained the thought of approaching Hiriko for help, but there would be no way a grieving widow would entertain requests from strangers. Rayna was still his best hope to help Daisy.

You want to see her again. A familiar voice crept inside his head.

"It's not about wanting to see her. I need to see her."

You like her.

Ari frowned. "We need her. Without her, our cub will die. Do you understand that?"

What will you do if she doesn't come?

He really didn't know. Rayna wasn't just his best hope; she was the last. His plan for the future hung in the balance. He placed a lot of hope on the what-ifs. Mr. Black had seemed so certain that the tragedy of losing her father would entice Rayna's caladrius forward. What if he was wrong?

"I'll do whatever I need to do to save our cub."

His phone burst into life. The tone had been changed to an annoyingly catchy pop tune. He couldn't help the smile that spread across his face. Daisy had been playing with his phone earlier. Ari made a mental note to change it later.

"Hello?"

"Is this Ari?"

The sound of her voice filled him with hope. A dangerous emotion at the best of times. "Rayna, it's good to hear from you. How are you doing?"

"I'm okay, I was wondering if the offer of dinner is still available?"

"What changed your mind?"

"My grandmother and uncle. There isn't much for me to do at the moment, and a change of scenery will do me a world of good. At least that's what my grandmother said."

"It doesn't sound like you agree."

She sighed, and the sadness in one single sound was almost tangible. "My mum still isn't herself. I'm worried about her."

"We can always meet up on a different day." He needed to see her, to start creating a bond because trust wasn't built on nothing. It wasn't built on a bunch of lies, either.

"It's okay. At least she isn't by herself, and my grandmother's right. There isn't much I can do while she sleeps."

"And what about her parents?" Hiriko's parents lived in China. Ari knew the relationship between them wasn't brilliant.

"It's complicated. I don't think anyone's told them yet. My grandmother thinks there's a chance they were involved somehow." She groaned, a surprisingly sexy sound that shot right to his groin. The intense reaction took him by surprise. "I'm sorry. I shouldn't have said that. We don't actually know."

"It's already forgotten." He filed away the information for later. There were a lot of questions surrounding Adam Jensen's death. A part of him didn't want to dig too deep. He wasn't interested in the why or the how. However, another part of him, the Broker, didn't like unanswered questions.

"Thank you."

"When do you want to meet?"

"Tonight? I know it's short notice. You probably already have plans."

Ari glanced at the open noddle box and discarded chopsticks. "I could go out and eat. How about I come and pick you up?"

"That would be great." She told him the address, something he didn't need to make a note of. He already knew. "I'll see you at eight?"

"See you then." Ari put his phone down.

HENDRICKSON HAD OFFERED TO DRIVE HIM, BUT ARI HAD dismissed the idea. He needed to appear as normal as possible. The front door opened, and Rayna stepped outside. She waved at someone still in the house and then walked toward

Ari's parked car. Before she opened the car door, she turned and looked up at the house. Ari leaned forward slightly and noticed the light at the top floor. Was someone in the attic?

Everything came into sharp focus. There were plenty of advantages to being more than human. He was faster, with a keener sense of smell. He was built for the hunt. It also made him a dab hand at spotting the difference. He could pick out the smallest details with little effort. It had been a skill that made him a talented agent.

A woman with long white hair sat behind the attic curtain. Pretty and almost ghostlike behind the netting. There was a faraway look in her eyes like her body was there but her mind elsewhere. Rayna's mum. Ari knew how she felt. When Daisy's mum died, part of him had as well. His memories of that day had haunted him for years. Without his daughter, he would have given up a long time ago. There wouldn't have been anything to live for. For a second, her eyes snapped into focus. She noticed him, sitting in the dark of his car. Then her head dropped, breaking the line of sight. Had he imagined her intense stare?

Rayna opened the passenger seat door and sat down. Lavender, honeysuckle, and vanilla announced her arrival. Ari's mouth watered, as her scent reminded him of the best desserts.

Ours. Taste.

Ari's stomach twisted with need and hunger.

He hadn't known what to expect. Her dark hair was a mess of waves, the strands of white falling across her forehead, bringing attention to her dark eyes.

"Hey." Her voice was soft, delicate, and a wave of possession went through him.

"Are you hungry?"

"Starving," she said with a small smile.

He studied her for a moment. The jeans she wore were

smart, the fabric dark and well-fitted against long legs. Underneath her black fitted jacket was a collarless jade green shirt. Sexy knee-high boots completed the look. His original plan involved a restaurant and a couple of bottles of wine, but she didn't look like she needed alcohol.

She needed something else.

"I didn't really have anything suitable for a restaurant."

"You look great," he replied, a little too gruffly. He wasn't going to start focusing on how good she looked. That train of thought would only lead to trouble.

"Are you sure?"

He nodded and smiled. "Perfect. I know where we can go."

CHAPTER NINE

Her mum hadn't come out of her catatonic state, and nothing Rayna said appeared to reach her.

Her father's body had been collected, wrapped up in linens, and taken to the underwater cave. Rayna had wanted to join the pod but had ended up waiting on the edge of the lake alone. Ruth and Declan had joined the other members of the pod, swimming in their seal forms, and her mum remained in the attic. That had been her grandmother's suggestion. Hiriko wasn't in any fit state for guests or to view the funeral ritual.

There had been a lot of visitors. A few spent the night before returning to their homes in the morning. Declan was still there, his original room still available for him to use. Rayna had done her part but mostly spent time by herself. She had only met a few of the visitors before, and she had always found it difficult to connect with others.

The official police report had arrived the morning after the burial, and Rayna had been in a funk ever since she read it. It was officially ruled as an accident due to reckless driving. It should have brought all of them an ounce of peace, but it hadn't. Her dad wasn't a reckless driver.

"Why don't you call that man you traveled here with?" Ruth had suggested.

Rayna had talked to Ruth about Ari when she'd first arrived. Her grandmother wanted all the details of the rich gentleman from Orchard who'd given her granddaughter a lift on his private jet.

There hadn't been much to tell. All Rayna had really learned—besides where he lived—was that he had a daughter and had been married some years ago. When Ruth had asked, Rayna told her she didn't plan on meeting him, even though he'd asked.

Her grandmother had reassured her that she knew about Ari Averus, the reclusive shifter who lived in Orchard. Besides his time spent with the FUC, nothing bad had been connected to him. He was a shifter who helped human veterans. She had also promised to make a note of his license plate and told Rayna she could keep her location app on her phone.

"I don't want to leave you all."

Both her grandmother and her uncle insisted that she needed to get out and do something that felt normal. Life would have to move on eventually. Why not enjoy a night with a guy she found handsome?

The sight of Ari in his smart, sleek black car made her heart skip. *It's not a date.* Rayna didn't want to overthink it, but it wasn't easy. Before she entered the car, she glanced up at the attic window. There was a telltale shadow. Her mum was back in the rocking chair. Rayna waved, but there was no telling if her mum actually saw her.

It was a beautiful night. There wasn't much in the way of air pollution this far from the major cities. On the crest of the horizon, she noticed the sparkling lights of the nearest town. The villages weren't big and were mostly hidden from view.

"Where are you taking me?"

"My favorite place."

Rayna thought he would take her to one of the largest cities. The Lake District had quaint bars and inns dotted in each of the villages, but Rayna got the impression Ari preferred more upscale restaurants. A man who chartered his own plane and lived in Orchard obviously had a lot of money and likely expensive tastes. "Do you spend a lot of time here?"

"My home is here. I do travel a lot for work."

"That must be nice. Besides my time at the Academy, I haven't traveled a lot. Do you have a favorite town or city?"

He kept his eyes on the road. "It's hard to pick one. I discovered a lot of cities have something worthwhile to them, but I always miss home."

She repositioned herself in the car, studying his profile. "Me too. I studied in Nottingham before I went to the Academy, but I spent my summers here."

"What did you study?"

"Criminology with a minor in English Literature."

"Impressive."

So was he. He was dressed in a suit, the jacket unbuttoned to reveal a pristine white shirt with no tie. An aura of power came off of him in waves.

"What animal do you shift into?" Whatever it was, it was big. There was something comforting about that.

He raised an eyebrow, not taking his gaze from the road. "Guess."

She nibbled her bottom lip as she studied him in the dark. "You're not a wolf."

"Is that a guess?"

"No." She shook her head. "I do my best thinking out loud. Not a lion either."

"What makes you say that?" he asked, sounding curious.

"It's hard to explain, but it doesn't feel right to me."

"Interesting talent you've got there."

Rayna shrugged. "Not really much of one. I've always been good at reading people. It is one of the traits the Academy picked up on."

"You find it hard to take a compliment, don't you?"

His observation made her laugh. She wasn't about to unload a bunch of traumas on him. The tragic aspects of her life meant always looking in on a world she could never be a part of. She realized that she enjoyed spending time with Ari. She found him incredibly distracting, and she needed that right now.

"How much longer till we get there?" Her growling stomach made her temporarily drop the guessing game.

"You hungry?" He didn't mention anything about her changing the subject.

"Starving. My grandmother isn't a fan of takeaways."

He glanced off ahead of them. "We're heading over there." Rayna followed the line of his finger as he pointed at something. A singular road going between two trees. He took the turn, and the smooth road became cobblestones. Ari slowed his car as they bumped along.

"There's a restaurant around here?"

"Not really. Can you smell that?"

Her window was still open, and she breathed in deeply. "What's that?"

"The best burger bar within a thirty-mile radius. It's a well-kept secret, but I'll share it with you."

Rayna's stomach rumbled again. She actually felt more

comfortable eating here than at any of the restaurants she thought he might have taken her. Had that been the original plan, but he had changed his mind? She liked a man who thought on his feet. If she hadn't been attracted to him before, she would have been now.

"Thanks."

"You're not a vegetarian, are you?" He actually appeared a little worried. "I should have asked what you prefer. A restaurant has more options. Tell me now and we can go somewhere else."

Did her feeling comfortable matter that much to him? "I'm fine, Ari. I'm not a vegetarian, and I haven't had a decent burger in ages."

He smiled as he pulled into a parking space. "Then you're in for a real treat. Marcus knows how to make the best burgers."

They faced each other in the dimly lit car. The dark look in his eyes was either because he really wanted the burger or he liked what he saw in her. Rayna had always thought she was good at reading people, but at that moment, she wasn't sure. There was every chance that Tall, Dark, and Handsome was flirting with her and it was going straight over her head.

He reached across to her, tucking a loose strand of hair behind her ear. The simple touch sent a jolt of desire through her. His mouth curved into a different kind of smile. Darker, complementing the knowing look in his eyes. Shifters could smell desire, couldn't they? Rayna's face went hot. How could she have forgotten that?

"You like it when I touch you, don't you?"

She wanted to nod. She wanted to admit to wondering what it would be like to be kissed by him. She wanted to forget everything that was going on and every worry that crept into her head. Instead, she said, "I'm pretty hungry."

He raised his eyebrows. Then shook his head slightly as if

he couldn't quite believe what she said. She couldn't believe it either. "Then I better get you fed."

Ari got out of the car, and Rayna fought against the urge to knock her head against the dashboard.

I'm such an idiot.

CHAPTER TEN

HHE WAS LOSING HIS TOUCH. ARI OPENED THE CAR DOOR AND helped Rayna out. Her face still looked pink under the streetlights, and she didn't look at him. The scent of desire still lingered in the air. She fought against her desire for him.

Intriguing.

"How did you find out about this place? It's a little off the beaten path."

Ari remembered the cobblestone pathway and her knee-high boots. He stepped toward her, scooping her up into his arms and causing her to squeak in surprise. Parts of their bodies were pressed together, and a spark of awareness shot through him. He hadn't even thought about it. Instinct had taken over, and he had acted on it without a second thought.

"Why did you pick me up?"

He glanced down at her, and his breath caught in his throat as her eyes sparkled. *God, she's beautiful.*

"I thought you might hurt yourself on the cobblestones."

"So, you picked me up?"

"I could have slung you over my shoulder. Either way would have worked."

They hadn't moved yet. Her weight was comfortable. Her closeness stirred something deep inside of him, and his bear roared in delight at their closeness. He really did like her. "I could have walked."

He glanced down at her. *It shouldn't be this hard to gain her trust.* She liked him, and he hadn't even needed to manipulate her. "I can put you down. Do you want me to?" He squeezed her slightly and caught the conflict in her eyes. He walked them toward the stall, which was brightly lit by fairy lights. Round tables dotted the area, with umbrellas shielding the patrons when the weather took a turn for the worse. Ari sat her down, her scent teasing his nose.

Marcus Finch, the owner of Marcus's Deli, watched them with a bemused expression on his face. Ari still remembered the day he'd stumbled across the stall when he had been in bear form. It had been closed, but the smell had been tantalizing. The following day he visited in the middle of the day and had his first of many burgers. It quickly became his favorite place to eat.

"You don't usually carry women around, Mr. Averus."

He smiled at the older man. "I didn't just randomly pick her up. I said I was going to treat her to the best burgers in the city. That place was closed, so I brought her here instead."

There was a second of silence, and then the man laughed. "You tell Marcus who sells better burgers than me and I'll send my wife over to have words with them." He picked up a rolling pin and tapped it against his hand. Rayna watched them, her eyes wide, a little taken aback by the random threat of violence.

"How's Isabella?"

"Fine, thank you. Now, tell Marcus what you'd like this fine evening."

Ari shot a look at Rayna, who remained perched on the table. They were the only couple there. "Anything you don't like?" She shook her head. "Then I'll have three of the specials. Two cold ones as well."

The man tsked in disapproval. "You know I don't like it when my patrons drink and drive."

"I promise I'm just having one." The elderly man liked to keep an eye on his clientele, but Marcus didn't have any knowledge of the supernatural world. There was no way he could know it took an obscene amount of alcohol for a shifter to get drunk.

"You better. It's a long walk from my tiny stall to your home in Orchard. Don't make me take your keys."

Ari raised three fingers; he'd never been a Boy Scout, but he knew the gesture. "You have my word, Marcus."

The man studied him for a moment, like he was trying to read the truthfulness in Ari's words. Whatever he heard in his tone seemed to appease him. "Then take a seat with your lovely lady, and I'll work my magic." He bent and pulled two beers free from the fridge kept underneath his counter. With an expert flick, the bottle tops came off in his hand. He handed the bottles to Ari and turned his attention to the grill in front of him.

Ari took the bottles to Rayna and handed one to her. "I hope you don't mind beer." He really needed to get into the habit of asking what she liked. He just kept making decisions without a second thought. Thankfully, she didn't appear bothered by him taking control. Or if she did, she didn't feel comfortable telling him to stop. He leaned toward the first idea.

"Are you okay?"

He noticed Rayna watched him from her spot on the table. The concern in her eyes was easy to read. He'd become completely lost in his thoughts.

"I'm fine. Any closer to guessing what kind of animal I am?"

She took a deep pull on her bottle and then flicked her tongue out to catch the last droplet around the rim. Ari didn't know if the move was deliberate, but the sight was sexier than it should have been. *I guess she likes beer.* He sat next to her legs. She was still sitting on the table, and he fought against the urge to run his hand up the length of her boot.

"Bear."

He thought it would take her longer. "How did you guess?"

"I ruled out the smaller breeds because there's nothing small about you. You have an aura about you. Like I would be able to sense you before you even walked into a room." She took another drink, and he noted the faint tremor in her hands.

"You noticed all of that?"

She shrugged. "You also ordered three burgers for the two of us. I like to eat, but I think one might be my limit here."

"Good observation skills."

She glanced around. Though they were the only people there, there was still a rumble of traffic somewhere close. The hidden burger stall would get busy soon. Ari wasn't a fan of crowds or strangers. He always thought it was tied to his days as an agent. Being surrounded by people was exhausting. Marcus's burgers were worth a little discomfort though. "It's nice here."

"It's one of my favorite places. It's popular enough to keep Marcus in business and a little off the beaten path so I don't have to fight anyone for my lunch."

"Do you want to take a stab at guessing my animal?"

"I'm not very good at guessing." Was she searching for the opportunity to tell him the truth?

"Can't your bear sense anything?"

Only that he wants to lick every part of you. He rubbed the bridge of his nose. "He's a little distracted."

"With what?"

"You," he replied honestly. Her eyes widened in surprise, and the smell of her desire filled his nose. *Damn, she smells good.*

"Here are your burgers. I wrapped up the third one. Considering how much you eat, I'm always surprised you're not the size of a horse." Marcus put two trays down and then patted his impressive stomach. "All I need to do is look at food and I gain five pounds. Isabella wants to get me onto one of those fancy keto diets. I don't see the point of it."

"Do you have kids?" Rayna asked.

Marcus smiled at Rayna. "Four. All monsters. They don't live with us anymore."

"Sounds like your wife wants you around to see any future grandkids."

"Of course."

Ari could sense the wave of sadness that came from her. Even Marcus's smile dropped when he caught sight of the way her dark eyes shimmered. Ari gestured to him to leave them. He got the impression Rayna didn't like it when people saw her upset.

A tear trickled down her cheek. Suddenly she started to study her food like it was the most important thing in the world.

The burger was double stacked with American cheese, crispy smoky bacon, and lettuce. To anyone else, it would have looked like a normal burger, nothing special at all. They'd be wrong.

"It might not look like much, but that first bite will change everything," he said, making conversation so she wouldn't feel bad for feeling her emotions. "The sauce is amazing. I'd offered to buy the recipe, but Marcus is taking it to his grave."

"I was expecting something bigger," she said with a small, bemused smile. He found himself grinning again. There was nothing fake about it. In that moment he wasn't trying to win her over.

"Shh, don't let Marcus hear that. You'll get the whole speech of not making judgment calls before you take a bite."

She brushed the back of her hand against her cheek. "I'm sorry. I don't usually cry in front of strangers."

"Rayna, it's been a rough couple of days for you and your family. I don't mind if you want to cry on my shoulder for a bit."

With nimble fingers, she picked up the burger and took a bite. Ari caught the precise moment the sauce touched her tongue. Her eyes went round, and she started to nod. "This is really good. Oh my God." Her words were muffled by the mouth full of food, and she picked up a napkin, hiding her mouth and her blush. "That is so embarrassing. I don't usually talk with my mouth full. I swear."

Ari shrugged. "I'm a bear, Rayna. I've got no problem with you enjoying your food. It's a little hot, not going to lie." He leaned forward. "It's also suddenly becoming my new favorite thing to see you blush. You look very pretty in pink."

CHAPTER ELEVEN

RAYNA ENJOYED HER TIME WITH ARI. THE CONVERSATION HAD flowed easily between them, and he managed to skirt around any awkward subjects. Even her short breakdown had been swiftly averted.

Rayna couldn't believe how close she had come to bursting into tears in front of two strangers. She knew she had a good reason, and she wouldn't be moving on toward healing while she still waited for answers. Was it a tragic accident, a rival pod, or her mum's parents? She didn't want to believe they were capable of murder, but they weren't the easiest people to love either.

"Did you enjoy the food?"

"I did, thanks for this."

"You don't need to thank me. I'm glad you called. How's your mum doing?"

"It's hard to explain. It's like she's trapped at the top of a tower and I can't reach her." Marcus had collected their trays a while ago. When he returned, he placed two steaming cups of coffee in front of them. "Thank you, Marcus."

The older man smiled at her; her earlier outburst had

been forgotten. He went back to his food stall. "Do you know many shifters who had to survive the death of their mate?"

He nodded. "It can take a while."

She had a couple of weeks before she needed to return to the Academy. That didn't feel like much time at all. "My grandmother's mate was murdered. Being pregnant with my dad helped."

"How's she's dealing with all of this?"

"By focusing on figuring out what happened."

Ari frowned. "You don't think it was an accident?"

She leaned forward, making sure to keep her voice low. "I know I'm not a fully trained agent, but there are lots of things about this that don't make sense."

"Hm." He sat back and studied her closely. "Your dad was a part of the Jensen Pod? That makes you a seal, right?"

It was a clever idea for him to change the subject. Every time her mind drifted, trying to figure out the why behind her dad's death, the urge to cry and never stop threatened to overwhelm her.

"He was, but I'm not."

"So, your animal is linked to your mum's side of the family?"

"It's a little more complicated than that."

"Adopted?"

She shook her head. "I'm definitely my parents' daughter. Actually, I should just tell you. I don't have an animal to call."

He watched her for a moment. "I don't think that's true."

"Are you calling me a liar?"

"Of course not." He appeared surprised at the disbelief in Rayna's voice. "Come on. Let's go for a walk, and then I'll take you back home."

She knew why his words had riled her. Rayna had suffered a lot of crap through her school days, including bullies who teased her relentlessly. The worst had been Victoria, a cat shifter who had accused Rayna of lying about being unable to shift. She claimed Rayna was making it up for attention.

Right, because lying about something like that was the quickest way to make friends and fit in.

Like high school wasn't hard enough.

She couldn't figure out why Ari was interested in her. Especially now that he knew she was a mongrel and she'd accused him of calling her a liar. Why wasn't he making excuses to get away from her? She wasn't strong or powerful. There was no way his bear would be interested in someone like her.

Oh well, at least the food and conversation were good.

They walked in silence. He probably wanted to end the night but couldn't figure out how to do it without coming off as a judgmental idiot. That was why he suggested the walk. Rayna should have said she was tired, save both of them the pains of a long and uncomfortable goodbye. She stepped toward the bridge. It wasn't big. It was quite small and quaint, made from big blocks of rounded bricks.

She walked onto the bridge and looked over the side into the water. Lanterns hung from the top of stands. Brilliant bursts of color were reflected in the water. It was hard to believe that her dad was somewhere in the depths, Not here. The caves were in the center of the lake. It wasn't a nice task to transport the bodies down there. Pollution was very much a thing.

Ari stood next to her. "How did you end up in the Academy?"

"When I'm a mongrel?" she snapped back, and then she

sighed. "I'm sorry. I was bullied a lot when I was younger. I'm still dealing with it."

"It's okay, Ray. You don't have to explain anything to me."

"Well, you did ask."

"I just wanted to know more about you."

Rayna turned around, only barely aware that Ari had called her Ray. Not many people called her that. Friends and family. She didn't have many of them either. She was tempted to open up to Ari but wary enough to remember she shouldn't be giving out FUC information. Including why they might have let a non-shifter into their training program.

"It's been a nice night. Can you take me back home?"

He moved from her side and in front of her. She didn't look up, but she could feel him there. Touching but not touching. There was a slight pressure on her chin, and he guided her face up. She didn't offer any resistance. She caught a flash of awareness in his gaze; his eyes turned gold. His animal stalking beneath the surface.

"Who are you?"

He traced a path across the line of her chin, and she shivered. "You know who I am."

She fought against the urge to roll her eyes. *Answer a question with a question.* His touch was distracting though, and she found herself moving toward him. *Is this how a magnet feels? I don't think I can move away from him.*

"You know I'm defective, broken."

His hold tightened, and his expression hardened. "I don't want to hear you call yourself that. You're not broken. I can feel you." Something stirred inside of her. A thing without words. "We can feel you." His lips brushed against hers, and she moaned. His arm went around her waist, and she was pulled hard against him.

Rayna knew they weren't alone, but for the life of her, a

herd of elephants could have run past and she wouldn't have heard them.

Damn, he knows how to kiss. Is he growling?

Everything about the man screamed controlled. The suit. The way he moved. Had kissing her made him lose it? A thrill went through her at the thought. He had eaten with relish, enjoying his burger. She liked the idea she was something he enjoyed. The way he kissed her, her soft body pressed against his hard one. Her whole body grew hot. The kiss continued, and she gave herself over to it.

Safe.

CHAPTER TWELVE

ARI HAD ENTERTAINED THE IDEA OF SEDUCING HER AS THE quickest way to gain her trust. After everything she had gone through, he figured it would be a line he didn't cross. Then he had given into temptation and kissed her.

The way she moaned as he claimed her mouth was the sexiest sound he had ever heard. Powerful enough to silence his inner voice and leave him wanting more. He held her close, losing himself in the feel of her soft body against his. Every ounce of self-control vanished in that moment. Ari didn't want the kiss to end.

"We should stop," she mumbled against his lips.

A pang of displeasure hit him. He didn't want to stop, and by the way she continued to kiss him, neither did she. Instead, he lifted her off her feet, enjoying her gasp of surprise. He wanted her to wrap her legs around his waist, until there was no space between them. *Claim her. Bite her. Ours.* His bear urged him on. The animal's intense reaction took him by surprise. His bear never reacted like this with Becca.

He lowered Rayna to the ground, breaking the sweet contact with her lips, and brushed a kiss against her forehead.

For a moment they looked at each other. Her skin was flushed, and her pupils were the only thing he could see. "Wow." It was a stupid thing to say but also the only thing he could say. He'd never experienced a kiss quite like the one he'd shared with her.

"I think you stole my line," Rayna said, looking up at him. Her strands of white hair reflected the colorful lights draped across the bridge, making her look impish. "Not that I'm complaining, but why did you kiss me?"

His heart still raced, and he placed her hand against his chest. "I kissed you because I wanted to. I might be a little rusty."

Her lips curved into a smile, and he could feel the heat coming from her. "Oh no. I give that ten out of ten. I have no suggestions on how you could improve on that."

Her depressing train of thought had been successfully derailed. He didn't know why her mental state mattered to him so much. "Good." He brushed another kiss against her forehead, tasting the warmth there. Her scent was delicious and tinged with desire. *Does she taste like honeysuckle everywhere?* Honey had been the downfall of many a great bear.

"I really should be heading home now." She sounded reluctant.

"I have work to do before tomorrow," Ari told her. "But if you're free, I'd love to see you again."

"I'd like that too."

He offered her his hand. The tightness in his chest eased as she slipped her hand into his. *Bite. Kiss. Claim. Ours.* Ari did his best to ignore his bear. Rayna shouldn't be a temptation. She was a means to an end, but for the first time in forever, Ari wished they had met under different circumstances.

RAYNA HAD STARTED TO TAP HER FOOT, A BALL OF NERVOUS energy. Ari found himself glancing in her direction. The roads were like a bowl of spaghetti but easy enough to navigate. Orchard could be found near the top of the lakes, to the east Redfield, and Poppyfield could be found on the west side of the lakes. It had been a deliberate choice of the shifters who had founded the villages. Too many shifters in one place might draw unwanted attention. There wasn't any need for him to travel or visit the other villages, but he knew the signs he needed to look for. The villages weren't clearly marked on any map, but there were markings for those who knew where to look for them.

I really want to kiss her again.

Which was why he couldn't. The game he played was dangerous, and while he knew he was the bad guy, he found out he was in no rush to break her heart.

She started to tap her foot again and brought his attention to her knee-high boots. An image flashed into his mind. Rayna in his guesthouse, completely naked other than the boots. He would thrust into her welcoming heat as she moaned his name. Ari didn't think he had boot kink, but the fantasy made him hard. At least it was dark in the car, and she couldn't see the effect she had on him.

There wasn't any way she could have missed how much he enjoyed kissing her, though.

He turned into the borough where her grandmother lived. Soft lights glowed from several of the homes. As they neared Ruth's house, he saw the light was still on at the topmost point. Rayna had mentioned her mother was staying in the guest room in the attic. Ari parked his car and turned it off.

"Can you help?"

He frowned. Her words didn't make any sense. "Help with what?"

She sighed. "My dad."

"You want me to find out if he was murdered?"

"Yes. My grandmother doesn't want to get FUC involved until we know for sure who it was. You must have old informants. People who could know something."

Kya's already searching for Mr. Black. If she can find him, then we could question him. I can't help but think he knows more than what he was saying.

Out loud he said, "There are a few people I could ask, but you shouldn't get your hopes up. I've been out of the game for a long time. There's a good chance my informants are dead or in prison. You could go straight to the FUC."

"Ruth thinks Mum's parents are behind it. She can't accuse them without proof because, if we're wrong, it won't end well."

"True. I'll see what I can find out on my end. Did your father have any enemies?"

"No." She sounded tired. "My dad ran a small fishing shop up in Perth six months out of the year. The other six months they lived in China. Everyone liked him. The only people who didn't were Mum's parents."

"Why did they hate him?"

"Because my parents were mates. Because their joining meant the purity of the bloodline was muddled. I was the next direct descendant of my mum's family. The next caladrius." She glanced out of the window and up at the house. "Mum was supposed to marry a distant cousin. That would have ensured proper offspring."

Rayna was starting to trust him. The things she had told him weren't public knowledge, and Ari would know.

"That's why you can't shift."

She nodded. "I've inherited some talents, like the ability to heal myself, but I don't have an animal. That can happen to some kids born to mismatched shifters. Not all the time but there are documented cases."

And there were others who died.

He leaned across the space between them, and Rayna moved closer. Their kiss was sweet, but he suspected it wouldn't take much for things to get heated. He pulled away and then rested his forehead against hers.

"You're beautiful, Ray." The words left him like they had a life of their own. As soon as he said them, he didn't want to take them back. He had the distinct impression she had endured a lot of shit and hadn't heard those words enough. He leaned in for another kiss, and as she moaned, he tasted her further. Coffee and a sharp tangy mustard. The combination shouldn't have worked, but his bear liked it. Another growl rumbled in his chest.

Suddenly her hand was on his chest, and she nudged him away. He groaned in disapproval.

"I'm a little old to be making out in my grandmother's driveway." Her words were breathy, and his stomach tightened in need. Her desire was thick in the air. Rayna had enjoyed that kiss as much as he had.

"You're never too old for that," he replied with a chuckle.

"Will I see you again?"

"That's on you. I'm not the one leaving in a couple of weeks."

"Tomorrow?"

He fought against the urge to feel relieved. "Come to my place for dinner."

"Okay."

He watched as she glanced at the house and observed the barest flicker in her eyes. A glow that appeared and disappeared so quickly that only another shifter would have seen it. Ari didn't know if she knew she had done it, but it told him one thing: Mr. Black was right. Rayna's caladrius was awakening.

He didn't want to rush her, but they were both running out of time.

CHAPTER THIRTEEN

Rayna woke up happy, which was odd. She didn't feel comfortable with it at all. Her lips were swollen from their stolen kisses in his car, and her whole body tingled with the memory. She could count on one hand how many people she had kissed. Ari blew all of them out of the water. He'd taken his time nibbling her lips and kissing the curve of her neck until Rayna thought she might combust.

And you're going to be seeing him again. At his house.

The thought terrified and thrilled her in equal measure. The way her body reacted to him was enough to make her heart race and leave her sweating profusely. She'd never had sex before, but she wasn't naïve enough to think they wouldn't be having sex when she got to his house. She wanted him on a level that scared her.

Rayna made her way down to the kitchen and made two cups of coffee. She peered out into the garden and caught sight of Declan. He sat under one of the garden umbrellas, scrolling through his phone. His expression was pensive.

She still hadn't gotten over the shock of seeing him. Even with the years between them, the similarities between him and his brother were unsettling. The sharp pang of pain was unmistakable. In the right light, she could have mistaken him for her dad.

It's probably for the best if Mum doesn't see him.

She leaned against the kitchen table, closing her eyes. They needed answers. Her grandmother had left the house early. Rayna wished she had taken her along. She could help with the investigation. But her grandmother wanted to keep her safe, even if Rayna didn't think she was at any risk of getting hurt.

She took the cups upstairs, taking the back stairs up to the attic.

Her mum was back in her chair like she had never left. Rayna put the cups down and knelt to face her.

"You're looking a little better."

Her hair was straight, and there was color in her cheeks. The vacant fifty-mile stare was still there. Had she combed her own hair, or had Ruth done it for her? Rayna gingerly reached out and brushed the back of her hand across her mum's cheek. Her mother didn't even react.

Is this what Ruth meant by slipping into the void?

"Did Gran see you this morning?"

No answer.

"She had some work to do. Don't suppose she told you where she went?"

Of course, she wouldn't have.

"I wish you would talk to me." She slumped onto the floor. "It's hard to stay positive, but I'm trying."

She picked up her cup and scooted near her mother's feet. "I've got no one to talk to about this."

I have Ari. He wanted to talk to me. He seemed really interested in what I had to say.

He seemed really interested in kissing me, Rayna corrected.

She really did like him, even if she barely knew him. He seemed to want to know all about her.

"I've met someone. I know the timing sucks, but there's something about him. I think you'd like him."

The kiss had stirred something inside of her, something that didn't have words, and she really didn't understand it. She really wished she had her mother to talk to about it.

"I'm being selfish," she whispered. "I shouldn't be spending time with him. I should be helping you. Goddess, what kind of daughter am I?"

"A good one."

For a split second, she thought her mum had spoken, but it was Ruth. Her grandmother stood by the open bedroom door. "I can't reach her. If I was any good, she would hear me."

Her grandmother entered the room and offered her hand. There was a look of utmost kindness on her face but steely resolve as well. "She's in a place no one can reach. Give it time."

"Did you learn anything while you were out?"

Her grandmother took Rayna by the hand. "I'll be back in a couple of minutes, Hiriko."

HER GRANDMOTHER KEPT SECRETS. RAYNA KNEW AND ACCEPTED that. As the alpha of the Lake District pod, she had a lot of people who relied on her. It didn't mean she was closed off or unapproachable. Her people trusted she would do whatever she had to in order to keep them safe. Rayna trusted her as well, but she hated secrets. She just hoped this wasn't one of those times when Ruth would keep some information close to the vest.

Once they returned downstairs, the older woman tapped

on the window, got Declan's attention, and gestured for him to join them.

When Rayna and Declan were seated around the kitchen table, Ruth. collected a bottle of scotch from a cupboard under the sink. Rayna watched as she poured out three measures of amber liquid and placed glasses in front of her and Declan. She shared a look with her uncle, but he looked as bewildered as she felt. Neither of them commented on the earliness of the day in regard to the alcohol. Rayna steeled herself for the worst.

"What did you find out?" Judging from the look on her grandmother's face, it wasn't good news.

"Someone cut through his brake lines."

Rayna picked up her glass and downed the harsh drink in one swift gulp. It burned a path down her throat and rested in the bottom of her stomach. Her eyes watered, and she fought against the urge to cough or throw up.

"Are you sure?"

The older woman nodded. "I was told the cut was clean."

Declan leaned forward. "The car went over undergrowth. How can they be sure the lines were cut?"

Her grandmother glared at him. "I trust our people, but a mechanic also confirmed the information."

Rayna picked up her coffee cup and took a sip. "It's time to get the FUC involved."

"I'm not sure about that," Declan said. "I still don't think we know everything. You said it yourself, Mum. Adam didn't have any enemies. Now you're saying the brake line was cut?"

"I've seen proof, Declan. This isn't the time or place for you to start questioning me. Someone deliberately attacked the pod. There's no telling if Adam was the only target or if we can expect more attacks."

Declan looked embarrassed. "We can't jump to conclusions without proof or a motive. This could lead to war. We all know it. Don't we?"

"Then we need to find more proof," Ruth said firmly.

"And how do we get that?"

"The only people who hated Adam were Hiriko's parents. Rayna could reach out to them." Declan suggested.

Ruth scoffed. "That's stupidly dangerous. If they were behind it, they'd know we're up to something. I won't risk her."

"Then how about me?" Declan suggested. "I could track them down, find some proof. I'm expendable."

For a second it looked like Ruth was actually considering it. Rayna caught a look of anger flashing across her uncle's face. He must hate it. Declan had never wanted to be in charge.

"Should I try asking Ari for help again?"

"Who's Ari?" her uncle asked, his momentary anger at his situation replaced with curiosity. "The man you went on a date with?"

"Do you think he'd help?" her grandmother asked.

"Who will help? Can someone please tell me who we're talking about?" Declan's expression had turned exasperated.

"The man she went on a date with. He worked with the FUC."

"Do we really want to bring a stranger into this?"

"Would you rather we risk you? Ari was trained for things like this, and he's more than capable of looking after himself." She looked at her grandmother. Shifters aged slower than regular humans, but in that moment, Ruth looked her age of eighty-two. "You don't want us to bring in the FUC, but I've asked for Ari's help before. He's already said he would consider it."

Her grandmother's attention was on the contents of her cup as she swirled it around. "It wouldn't hurt, but you have to make sure it doesn't get back to the FUC. If the people behind your dad's death know we're on to them, they might scatter or destroy any evidence linking them to the car crash." As she reached out, Rayna met her halfway, holding her hand. "Be careful."

"I will. I promise."

CHAPTER FOURTEEN

KYA STILL HADN'T GOTTEN IN CONTACT WITH ARI. THE LAST time he had spoken to her had been a couple of days ago. She had suggested trying to track down the elusive Mr. Black and promised she would be careful. Now she wasn't answering her phone. Ari spent the morning calling old contacts, asking for them to get back to him if they heard anything about Kya. When he was finished, he put the phone down and leaned back in his chair.

He hadn't been able to get last night out of his head. The way Rayna had kissed him back, her sweet moans, and the automatic way she pressed her body against his. A heady combination that made him feel like he was going to lose his mind.

He wasn't some wide-eyed virgin, but what he experienced with her was something completely new. Now he had unanswered questions. He hated unanswered questions. Her request for help had snuck into his mind and stayed there. He wanted to help her.

Daisy sat on the futon, a selection of coloring books in front of her. Ari had braided her hair before he had started work, and while he knew she needed to be resting, he hadn't been able to refuse her when she asked to keep him company. Hendrickson had made her a ham sandwich, divided into four with the crusts cut off.

She had nibbled at them, but that was it.

How long do we have left?

He didn't want to dwell on it, but he was putting a lot of faith in a woman he barely knew and an event that may or may not occur. What if Mr. Black was wrong and Rayna continued to be unable to reach her caladrius? Ari pushed the thought to the back of his mind; he couldn't think of it like that. He didn't have a choice.

He glanced back down at the papers. Screenshots of his office security feed. They were state-of-the-art and never failed, but they had gone offline for the entire time Mr. Black was in his office. Ari didn't believe in coincidences.

He had the distinct impression he was being played.

"I should have killed him."

"What, Daddy?"

"Nothing, sweetheart. Just work stuff."

"Henny said hurting people is wrong."

Ari looked up from his desk. Hendrickson was a beast of a man. A bear shifter whom Ari had met during his brief time as a specialist in the army. He had been the first bear shifter he'd seen in months. It was strange to have friends, as he had always known fewer personal ties between him and others was for the best. Hendrickson was tall, broad-shouldered, with white hair, short on the sides and longer on the top. His body was covered in scars, something that shouldn't have been possible for a shifter. Their kind could heal a lot of physical damage, but there were limits. The large man would lay down his life for the little girl on the futon. "What if it's the only way to protect someone you love?"

"I'd find another way," his daughter said with a certainty

only a child possessed. She bit her bottom lip as she focused on her coloring sheet. A dog maybe or a muddy-looking fox?

"You're smarter than most people."

She giggled, and a weight lifted from his chest.

His phone burst to life, and he quickly looked at the number on the screen. He pushed the green button. "I didn't think I would be hearing from you so soon. We said five, didn't we?"

"We did. I really need to talk to you. Are you available to meet sooner?" She sounded tired.

"Are you okay?"

There was a moment of silence, and for a second, he thought she had hung up. Then she sighed, and he could hear all the pain she kept buried. "Please, Ari. I really need to see you. I wouldn't ask if it wasn't important."

He looked across at his daughter. He'd thought he had a little more time before Rayna's arrival. He didn't want to tell her no, especially considering that the sooner she was here, the sooner the next step of his plan could kick into gear. "Okay, I'll get my driver to collect you."

There was another long drawn-out pause. "You have a driver?" she asked in disbelief.

"His name is Hendrickson. He's more family than staff. He doesn't warm quickly to strangers, so don't take anything he says personally."

"Okay."

"He'll head over to get you now. I'll see you in a bit."

He switched the phone off and noticed that Daisy was staring at him curiously. "Who's coming?"

"Just one of Daddy's friends."

"You have friends?"

He clutched his chest, swirling in the chair like she'd hit him with an arrow. "Words hurt, little lady." He got to his feet and scooped his daughter up into his arms.

"Daddy's strong. He can handle it. Who's coming over?"

"Her name is Rayna. If you're a good girl, you'll get to meet her at some point. Come on. Let's go find Henny and get you ready for your nap."

———

As Hendrickson went to collect Rayna, Ari took Daisy back to bed. She hadn't wanted to go to sleep, especially not when they were going to have guests. He promised if she was a good girl, he would introduce her to Rayna. They just had boring, grown-up things to discuss first. Things Daisy wouldn't find interesting at all. For a second, he thought she might try and argue with him, but she yawned instead, hugged her teddy bear, and closed her eyes as he reattached the monitor to her arm.

He made his way back to his office and tidied up her coloring pencils and papers. Why did Rayna want to see him sooner? The purely male part of his mind thought it had something to do with the kiss. A more logical part figured it had something to do with her asking for help solving her dad's murder.

A murder she can't prove.

Did Ari want to get involved with that? It was a bad idea, but he no longer liked the idea of anyone hurting Rayna. He shouldn't care. He needed the complicated woman for only one thing, but the more he got to know her, the more he liked her. It was a slippery slope.

Ari sat at his desk and opened the top drawer. He couldn't remember the precise moment he hid the framed photo away. The photo was of Becca and Daisy, a few hours after their daughter had been born. The rabbit shifter looked tired but happy. The labor had been long and difficult, but it had been worth it to see the smile on her face as Daisy was laid on her chest. The photo always had a place of pride on his desk, until Becca was killed. Then he couldn't look at her smiling face anymore. It hurt too much.

Hopefully, one day he'd be able to tell Daisy all about the brave, fearless woman who'd been her mum. He just hoped Daisy would forgive him for failing her. With a heavy sigh, he slipped the photo away, putting the reminder of his old life back into the drawer.

I can't fall in love with her. Becca died because of me. I can't risk the same thing happening to Rayna.

CHAPTER FIFTEEN

The man who picked Rayna up introduced himself as Hendrickson, but he hadn't seemed interested in talking to her. Ari had warned her not to take anything the man said as personal, but for her to be offended, the man had to say something.

The journey from humble Redfield to Orchard took forty-five minutes around the lake. It wasn't cheap to live in Orchard. Either Ari came from money or he had invested well.

All of the gardens are well kept and beautiful, and many of the houses had gates—large steel ones. Hendrickson pulled the car up to one, reached out of the window, and typed in a code. The gate swung open, and they drove up the driveway.

"This place is huge for just one person. Ari must get lonely."

Hendrickson gave a noncommittal grunt as he parked the black sleek car.

"Not a fan of small talk?"

He looked at the rearview mirror. His eyes flared gold. Definitely a bear. "Mr. Averus doesn't have a lot of guests. There is no reason for idle chitchat."

"A man of a few words. I get that." There was a heavy sigh, but he didn't correct her. "Why doesn't he have a lot of guests?"

He frowned. "He likes his privacy."

But he had invited her. He had even let her come earlier than planned. Why?

It's pretty clear what he wants. The question is, am I going to give it to him? He's handsome and charming, and the kiss we shared made every nerve burn with an intensity I didn't think was possible. Even if I can't say the words out loud, I like him. I like him a lot.

And now I'm going to ask him for help.

She left the car when Hendrickson opened the door.

"I never would have guessed that. I mean the gate is so small and unassuming," She smiled. For a split second, she thought Hendrickson might smile back at her. It didn't happen, but was that an involuntary twitch?

"Why are you here?"

"You couldn't have asked that question in the car? That would have been better than the uncomfortable silence." Hendrickson continued to watch her. She sighed. "I need his help."

The tall man studied her. Ari had said the man was like family. Rayna had always believed in honesty being the best policy. There was every chance Hendrickson could smell a lie like Ari or could do something much simpler than that. Rayna had been trained to read a situation and person. It wasn't a unique skill and she got the distinct impression the bear shifter would refuse her entry if he thought she was a threat. Would he put her back into the car and take her home if he thought she was a danger? Could she solve the mystery of her dad's murder without Ari's help? That would mean involving FUC, and Ruth didn't want that.

Hendrickson still hadn't moved. It was like he was waiting for something.

"I also think he's pretty handsome," Rayna said with a shrug. Then she edged closer to the house. "Plus, we kind of kissed."

Hendrickson had been pale before, but he somehow grew paler. Did he have a problem with the altitude up there?

"Why are you still outside? I heard the car park minutes ago."

She looked up to see Ari had stepped out of the house. She couldn't help smiling at the sight of him. He was dressed in a pair of jeans and a blue shirt, the sleeves rolled up to reveal impressive forearms. Rayna pushed her nervousness to the pit of her stomach. She really didn't know him, and she was about to walk into the lion's den… no, the bear's den. "Hendrickson was just telling me about your beautiful garden."

Rayna knew he could detect the lie, but she also figured he had heard their one-sided conversation.

"He worked hard on it."

She glanced at Hendrickson in surprise "You're a gardener?"

"Among other things." The top of the man's cheeks went pink. "I like flowers."

"And I think they like you as well." She had written off the big guy as hired muscle, but he had hidden layers. That taught her to judge someone without getting to know them. "Your garden is beautiful, Hendrickson." She noticed as Ari hid his smile behind his hand. He seemed to enjoy seeing his friend flustered.

Hendrickson mumbled something that sounded like

thank you, followed by, "I'll go put the car into the garage." He returned to the car and drove away, going somewhere behind the house.

"I've never seen Henny look so flustered before."

"Henny?"

"It's his nickname," Ari said in explanation without really explaining at all.

He walked down the steps and stopped in front of her. There was a serious look in his eyes, and Rayna didn't have the strength or the will to stop him. He closed the distance between them and lightly touched her cheek before brushing his lips against hers. She fought against the urge to throw her arms around his shoulders and deepen the kiss. *You're in a world of trouble, Rayna.*

"It's good to see you."

"You saw me yesterday," she said with a smile.

"And I'm still happy to see you. Let's talk in my office."

IF ANYONE ASKED HER ANY QUESTIONS ABOUT ARI'S HOME, SHE wouldn't have been able to tell them the color of the carpet. She was a terrible agent. As soon as the thought passed through her mind, she dismissed it. Ari wasn't a target, so there was no reason she needed to remember details of his home.

They walked into his office, and Ari closed the door behind them.

Rayna gave in to temptation. All the times they had kissed, he had taken the lead but not now. She threw her arms around his shoulders and kissed him. He made a noise of surprise before he quickly took control. With little effort, he picked her up, and she wrapped her legs around his waist.

Those powerful arms of his held her in place. She couldn't seem to stop herself.

He moved her and sat her down on the edge of the desk, continuing the exploration of her mouth in the most mind-blowing kiss she had ever experienced, though she didn't have much to compare it to. Ari really, truly blew any past kisses clear out of the water.

"This is one hell of a hello," he said as he broke his contact with her lips and kissed a path down the curve of her neck.

Less talking. More kissing. Her inner voice spurned her on. She found his mouth again, threading her fingers through his thick, dark hair.

"I really want to sweep everything off my desk and take you right here."

She wanted that too.

Claim me. I'm yours. Mate.

Rayna froze. Where the hell did that come from? Was she that starved for affection that a couple of really good kisses were making her think crazy thoughts? Rayna wasn't a true shifter; she wouldn't have a mate.

"Are you okay?" Ari noticed her panic and stepped away from her. She wanted to grab him again. It took a great amount of will to stop herself.

Bite me. Mark me. Make me yours.

Rayna jumped off the desk. What the actual hell?

He's mine. Ours. Mate.

The strange voice wouldn't stop and it grew louder until she couldn't hear her own thoughts anymore. She squeezed her eyes shut, grabbing the side of her head. Her knees went weak, and she hit the carpet.

"Rayna, what's wrong?"

She could barely hear him over the chanting in her head. That wasn't her voice. People could control their inner monologues. A warmth spread over her like a blanket, but there was no weight over her. Ari knelt next to her, his inner animal comforting her. She felt it. She shouldn't have been able to, but she did. She knew his bear was reaching out to her.

Calm.

She opened her eyes and looked at Ari. "What's happening to me?"

"Tell me what you're feeling."

"My head hurts." It sounded dumb, but she couldn't explain it any other way. "It's so noisy."

"Rayna, we're the only ones here."

A lie. He just lied to us. Hendrickson was there, and the house was huge. Ari had to have other members of staff. *No. Can you smell that? A young one. A child.*

She couldn't believe she was arguing with herself. It had been a rough week, but was it enough to make her lose her mind?

I am yours; you are mine. He is ours.

"Who else lives here?"

He frowned. "You've already met Hendrickson."

"Anyone else?"

"I hire a cleaning staff who look after the house when I'm not here. That's it." A bitter acrid smell filled the air, and something like understanding dawned on his face as he read her expression. "You detected a lie."

He admitted the lie but didn't explain himself. Rayna frowned. "I've never been able to do that before." She didn't mention the voice in her head. Either she had lost her mind or it meant something else. Something that should have been impossible. Rayna needed to think about it, talk to her family.

Mate.

No, you have to be wrong.

I'm not. Her inner voice sounded insulted that Rayna had even questioned it.

"Who else lives here?" she asked again, more forcefully.

He stood and offered his hand. She slipped hers into his and let him help her up. "How about I show you? Then you can tell me what you need."

CHAPTER SIXTEEN

Ari hadn't meant to lose himself with her. He had every intention of letting her say what she needed to say. To offer his help if he could. He'd figured she must have discovered something about her father's accident. Hadn't she said something yesterday about her grandmother's investigation?

The tension as they walked down the hallway had bordered on unbearable. His bear had been in a state of hyperawareness Ari had never experienced before. Then he closed the office door, and she kissed him. His bear had roared in approval.

A strong mate.

Those words had sent a wave of terror straight through him. Those doubts were silenced as the kiss deepened. All the things he needed to do rushed out of his mind, and all he could think of was claiming her, marking her smooth skin with a bite.

Mate.

Then something happened. She had shoved him away and collapsed to the ground. Then she had done the unexpected, asking him, *Who else lives here?*

He had mentioned Daisy on the plane without much thought but hadn't brought her up to Rayna again. Ari had truly thought with everything that was going on in her life, she might have forgotten. While he planned on introducing them sooner rather than later, it coming up like this was strange. Had she remembered, or did this have something to do with the way she grabbed her head? Like she could hear something Ari couldn't.

All the trust they had built was on the verge of disappearing if he didn't do something, quick.

"How about I show you? Then you can tell me what you need."

The feel of her hand in his calmed something inside of him. Not for the first time his bear was in awe of her. He had never been that taken in this same way with Becca or her rabbit.

Ours.

He rubbed his thumb across her knuckles. Her breath caught at the contact. Then he led her to Daisy's bedroom.

"Why can't you just tell me?" She sounded worried.

"Because you asked for an explanation. It'll be easier to just show you." They came to a stop outside the bedroom door, and he opened it. He nodded at her, and she stepped past him, looking into the bedroom. He watched her face as she frowned at the bed then the dolls on the floor, the pink desk. Then she noticed the hospital equipment.

He gestured for her to return to the hallway so they could talk without disturbing Daisy. He quietly closed the door behind them.

"Who is she?"

Ari took a deep breath and sighed. "Her name is Daisy, my daughter. I mentioned her on the plane."

"I completely forgot."

"It's okay. You've got a lot going on, and there was every

chance we weren't going to see each other again. Why would you remember?"

She slumped against him, and he picked her up. She was light in his arms. For a second, he thought she might fight against him, but she didn't. Even in her confusion, she still trusted him. Ari walked them away from his daughter's bedroom and headed back to the kitchen.

"What's wrong with her?"

"She was born with a defect." He sat her down on a stool and collected a couple of glasses. Then he filled hers up with cool water and handed her the glass, noticing the faint tremor in her hands.

"And her mum?"

"Becca died when Daisy was a baby."

"And the defect?"

There was no way he could lie about it. Not now. "I'm a bear shifter. Becca was a rabbit. It's extremely rare, almost unheard of, but sometimes, mismatched shifters can produce offspring with the inability to thrive."

"Offspring of mismatched shifters. Like me."

Ari nodded. "Except she's dying because of it."

"Oh."

"Why did you ask to come here early?"

"I need to know if my grandparents are behind my dad's death."

"You think I can help with that?"

She reached out and took a hold of his wrist. "I do."

"And if they were behind it?"

"I don't know." There was an intense pain behind her dark gaze. Her eyes practically swam with unshed tears. "We know someone cut the brake cables. It was deliberate. I know there's no love between the families, but I hope it didn't come to this. This could destroy my mum completely if it's true."

"Then tell Ruth it isn't true."

"You want me to lie to her? I'm guessing you've never met her. That woman can read me like a book."

"Okay, you don't lie. You just let it go. Tell Ruth that nothing good is going to come from finding out who's behind your dad's death. She'll believe you."

"And then what about my mum? She sits in the attic; she doesn't drink or eat. She needs answers. It might be the only way to reach her." Rayna rubbed her forehead.

He couldn't bear to see her in pain, and a part of him cried out to help her. How was it possible she had become such an important part of his life in such a short amount of time? He knew he was desperate for her help with Daisy, but this feeling was more than that. A need to take away her pain. His animal's insistence to mark her, to claim her as theirs. That only meant one thing.

Mate.

The Goddess had a cruel sense of humor.

"Can you help me?"

He wanted to say no, but instead, he nodded. "I'll help you, Rayna."

The connection to her was deepening. He could read her emotions with ease. Now that she'd seen Daisy and learned about her illness, a weight was off his shoulders.

Now all he needed to do was ask her to try to heal Daisy.

Rayna looked relieved. Whatever was happening between them was too new, and neither of them really understood it. Ari also knew it couldn't be more than what it was. She had connections with FUC. Ari had already done that and had no plans to return. He enjoyed his life as the Broker.

"When my mum is better, I can tell her about Daisy. I know she'll be able to help."

"Daisy doesn't have that long." It pained him to say the words out loud. It was one thing to have them play on repeat in his head, but to say them to another person… It made everything more real.

Rayna frowned. "How long does she have?"

"Not long."

"I'm sorry, Ari. I can't even reach my mum at the moment. She's in no fit state to heal anyone."

He moved around the kitchen counter and plucked the glass out of her hands, putting it on top of the counter. She looked wary, and Ari couldn't blame her. The only reason why she hadn't discovered the truth was because she hadn't asked the right questions. And if he was right, something was changing inside of her.

Maybe Mr. Black was right about it being time for her caladrius to emerge but wrong about what would incite it. Her father's death hadn't, but maybe their kiss had.

"What about you?"

Her eyes widened slightly. "I don't have the caladrius. I can't heal anyone."

"Have you tried? You told me you could heal yourself. Maybe you just haven't learned you can use the ability on others."

She shook her head. "The times I managed to heal myself I've been unconscious."

Ari closed his eyes, and whatever hope he had felt was torn away from him. He leaned onto the kitchen counter and tried to calm his racing heart. He had come so far, but every time he thought he had an answer, it was gone in the blink of an eye. His bear roared to life inside of him. Daisy might not have been able to shift into a bear, but his animal didn't care. She was their cub no matter what.

Suddenly there was a pressure against his back as Rayna hugged him. He glanced down in surprise to see her arms around his waist. His bear stilled, and Ari followed suit. His inner turmoil slowly faded at the simple touch.

"I'm sorry, Ari."

"It's not your fault."

"I know. I wish I could help her, but I wouldn't even know where to begin."

Her presence behind him was comforting. "It's okay, Rayna."

He turned to face her, and Rayna leaned against his chest. He held her close, resting his chin on top of her head. He never thought he was that kind of man, but touching her brought him a measure of peace. His bear liked the feel of her in his arms. The world stilled around them.

"Everything's going to be okay." He wanted to believe those words, but he didn't.

CHAPTER SEVENTEEN

RAYNA AND ARI DECIDED TO CUT THEIR EVENING SHORT, AND Hendrickson drove Rayna back home.

Rayna hadn't known what to say to Ari. He had promised he would help her, but he had a lot to deal with in his own life. It had taken Rayna completely by surprise to find out he had an ill daughter. Her diagnosis was even more surprising. A child of mismatched shifters, like her, but one with a rare and seemingly uncurable disease? And here Rayna had thought not being able to shift was the worst possible outcome.

Ari had given her a sweet kiss and promised to call her in the morning.

The entire ride home, Rayna tried to think of ways she could help. One thing kept coming to mind: the fact that something was changing inside of her, and it wasn't as simple as losing her mind. She had never experienced anything like it before, a voice that wasn't hers, almost arguing with herself. It sounded insane. Was this something shifters experienced? Why was it happening now?

She really needed to talk to someone. Not Ari. If she told

him what she thought might be happening, he might think she could help Daisy, and she didn't want to give him false hope.

Ruth would have some answers. Or at least Rayna hoped she would.

Hendrickson parked, and Rayna got out of the car. "Thanks."

"Goodbye, Miss Jensen. It was a pleasure to meet you."

She was fairly sure it was the longest sentence the man had ever uttered. She made her way up the steps, unlocked the door, and entered the warm hallway. The house was mostly quiet, but Ruth wouldn't have left Rayna's mother by herself. Uncle Declan wouldn't have done it either.

"What did he say? Is he going to help us?"

The unexpected voice made her jump. She glanced up the stairs and noticed Uncle Declan sitting at the top, like he had been waiting for her. "He said that he would."

"I don't trust him." He continued to watch her from his place at the top of the stairs.

She hung up her jacket. "You don't know him."

"Neither do you, but you're more than willing to trust him."

"He used to be an agent for the FUC. That has to inspire at least some level of trust."

"And have you done any research on him? You're not just taking him at his word, are you?"

"I know he isn't lying." She was still shocked that she'd scented the small lie from him earlier. Was that proof that something had changed, or just a strange coincidence?

Her uncle sighed. "How, Rayna? "

Rayna gritted her teeth. Declan's tone made her want to pull back inside of herself. He had never made her feel that way before. He had always been one of her favorite people.

"I've been studying at FUCN'A. Do you think I might have learned a few things to help with my shortcomings?"

"I doubt it'll be enough." He sat with his hands together, most of his face cloaked in deep shadow. Before, she wouldn't have been able to make out any details on his face. Now she would see everything. The scowl. Something close to disgust in his eyes. Her new talent surprised her but so did her uncle's demeanor. Something must have happened to put him in a bad mood—which was rare for him. Uncle Declan was easygoing, but everyone was stressed at the moment.

"Where's Nan?" She had enough of this conversation. She knew that everyone was running on edge, so she tried hard not to take what he said personally.

"In her room. She made sure your mum had something to eat, and then said she wanted to have a rest."

"How's Mum doing?"

"No real change." An uncomfortable silence descended between them. He continued to watch her, and the hairs on the back of her neck stood on edge.

Bad man. The voice snuck into her mind.

Brilliant, it's back.

She found Ruth in her bedroom. The older woman was nestled on her bed, a book in her hands. She glanced up as Rayna walked in. She slipped a bookmark between the pages and patted the mattress. Rayna joined her, crossing her legs. "What did he say?"

"He'll help."

She smiled. "That's good news. Why don't you look happier?"

"I don't know how to say this, and I don't know if I should mention anything. It really doesn't compare to what's going on."

Ruth's smile faded, and she looked truly worried. It really

pained Rayna to add to Ruth's stresses. She already had so much on her mind. "What's wrong?"

"What does it feel like with your animal?"

Ruth frowned. "What do you mean?"

"This is going to sound insane, but I'm hearing voices. No. Not voices. Just one."

Ruth offered her hands, and Rayna held them. Ruth's eye color changed as her animal neared the surface.

After a moment, Ruth said, "That's amazing."

"What's wrong with me?"

"Nothing's wrong with you. I can sense something."

"What does that mean?" Rayna needed to hear someone say what should have been impossible.

Ruth dropped her hands and touched either side of Rayna's face, searching her eyes as if she could see deep into her soul. "Rayna, your animal has awoken."

"Are you sure?" Rayna was suddenly glad she sat down. "What kind?"

"I don't know, sweetheart." She leaned forward, still studying Rayna's gaze. "I can only tell you that I can sense it. What happened?"

Her cheeks burned as she remembered the kiss she shared with Ari in his office. The voice had mentioned a word that hadn't made any sense. Not to a non-shifter, anyway.

"I think Ari is my mate." She thought admitting it out loud would be like a weight being lifted off her shoulders, but it didn't feel that way at all. Instead, it felt weightier. More real. "But that's impossible, right? I don't have an animal. I don't have a mate."

"In this world, nothing is impossible. The goddess has brought you together for a reason. You shouldn't question divine will."

"But I'm a mongrel."

As soon as the word left her lips, she saw her grandmother's expression darken. "I've always hated that word. You are my granddaughter. Strong and powerful, finding her place in the world. I've always been proud of you, and I know both of your parents felt the same way. You've survived in a world that has little time for you."

"But you never wanted me to go to the Academy."

"I just couldn't bear the thought of you being hurt. Our world is dangerous, and being an agent makes it even more so. You've always been smart, Rayna."

"Do you think I could heal Mum?" That question had been preying on her mind since she heard the voice and suspected what it meant.

"I don't know, sweetheart. I don't know which animal is inside of you. I recognize you as part of my family and that means you could be a seal. It also means you're my granddaughter. You'll always be my family even if you take after your mother and have her animal."

Rayna lay on the bed, resting her head against her grandmother's legs. Rayna had always felt like an outsider in her family. She had always thought of herself as little more than human, but something was changing inside of her. The voice inside of her was an animal, a creature she might be able to shift into. That was all she'd ever wanted. To be like her family. "How do I find out which animal I inherited?"

Ruth ran her fingers through Rayna's hair. "The surest way is to talk to another of your kind."

"There isn't anyone I can talk to."

"That's not exactly true."

"Mum's not talking."

"I don't mean your mother." Her words were cryptic but Rayna knew who she was talking about.

She rolled onto her back and looked up at her grandmother. "We can't trust them. What if they were the ones who killed Dad?"

"We don't know that for sure. We also haven't told them what's happened. They might want to be here. To help Hiriko. She's their daughter, after all."

"Or they'll use it as an excuse to take her with them." And she would never see her mum again.

"And maybe that would be for the best. Her own mother might be able to heal her. "Ruth traced a pattern against Rayna's forehead. "I'm not saying we trust them, but you need guidance," she paused. "Unless."

"What?"

"You can try letting your animal talk to your mum."

THE PIT OF RAYNA'S STOMACH TWISTED INTO KNOTS AS RUTH led the way up to the attic. Rayna looked at the stairs as she followed, not knowing what to think or say.

The pressure and hope that built inside of her made her feel physically ill. She had barely had enough time to come to terms with the fact that something was changing, let alone the idea that, if she took after her mum, there was every chance she could heal her.

But if the caladrius had truly awoken, giving her the ability to heal, would she know how to use it?

"I don't think I'm ready for this."

"I know."

"What if it doesn't work?"

"Then we call your grandparents and see if Haru is willing to help. Then I'll help you connect with your seal."

Rayna touched her chest, feeling the beat of her racing heart. "Do you think she'll help?"

"She disowned your mother when she fell in love with Adam, but as a mother, I can't imagine not helping my child when they needed it." She opened the door at the top of the stairs and gestured for Rayna to enter first. It didn't matter how many times Ruth put Rayna's mum into bed, she always managed to find her way out of it again and back to the rocking chair.

Rayna rubbed her sweaty hands against the back of her jeans. A headache brewed just behind her eyes, and she took a deep breath.

"Mum?" No answer.

Rayna took a few tentative steps forward. She didn't know how she was supposed to deal with Hiriko in her current state. The person in the chair wasn't her mum, not really. There was no spark behind her eyes, and while she had always been pale, now it was even more noticeable.

Rayna moved in front of her, perching on the windowsill, and reached out, taking Hiriko's hands in hers. Cold and clammy.

"Try making eye contact." Ruth stood to the side.

"It's like she can't see anything." Rayna moved off the windowsill and knelt. "Mum?" Still nothing from Hiriko, but something stirred inside of Rayna. A coil of energy. It travelled down her arms, pooling into her hands. The sensation didn't have words, or if it did, Rayna didn't know what it was. If she hadn't been looking so closely at her mum, she would have missed the flicker in Hiriko's eyes.

The energy grew inside of her, and Rayna gasped.

"What is it?"

"I don't know," she replied breathlessly.

Ruth knelt on the other side of her mum, studying her face. "Hiriko, can you hear me?"

The energy twisted into something close to pain, and Rayna cried out. She wanted to let go. The pain would stop if she broke contact, but some color had returned to her mum's face.

It's working!

Hiriko's eyes flickered again. She looked left and then right. Neither of them missed it.

Family.

The pressure inside Rayna built to unbearable levels, and she couldn't bear it anymore. She pulled her hands free of her mum, squeezing her eyes shut and grabbing the sides of her head.

The darkness swallowed her, twisting her vision into a pinprick of light.

Then, everything changed.

CHAPTER EIGHTEEN

SOMETHING'S WRONG.

A sudden spike of pain at the base of his skull made Ari pause mid-step. He didn't know the precise reason for the blinding pain, but his bear roared in displeasure.

Ari leaned against his desk and with his free hand rubbed the sore spot. Something was wrong with Rayna. It had to be the reason for this sensation, but what was happening to her?

He picked up his phone, selected her number, and waited. Nobody answered, and the uneasy feeling grew. He stood, grabbed his jacket, and called out to Hendrickson.

"What's wrong?" the bear shifter asked, poking his head out of the kitchen.

"I'm not sure, but I need to see Rayna." At his friend's frown, he asked, "What?"

"You're getting awfully close to her. Do you think that's a good idea?"

"Not even a little bit, but it's complicated. If Daisy wakes up, tell her I'll be home soon." And with that, he closed the door and jumped into his car.

He tried hard not to break any speed limits in his rush to

get to Rayna. He pushed the limit a little, but his irritation spiked every time he was forced to stop at a red light. Goddess, it was so strange. The impending feeling of doom threatened to override his common sense. He knew it didn't have anything to do with him but everything to do with her. What had happened in the hours since he'd last seen her?

And what was the connection that burned brightly between them?

Mate.

"No, it can't be that. Becca was my mate." But even as he said it, he corrected himself.

She was our wife but never our true mate.

Ari parked his car, the engine barely switched off before he leaped out of it. He took the steps two at a time and banged on the door.

Let me out.

"Wouldn't make a good first impression if we broke down the door."

I don't care, his bear replied stubbornly.

Thankfully, it didn't come to that. The door opened, and an older woman with white cropped hair answered. Ruth Jensen, the head of the Redfield seal pod. She was dressed in a long white robe, but on her feet were black boots and she carried a flashlight. That was when Ari noticed the broken glass on the ground.

"It's a little late for guests. Come back in the morning."

As she closed the door, he jammed his foot forward, stopping her. "Where's Rayna?"

"How do you know my granddaughter?"

"My name is Arimas Averus. I'm her mate." The words felt weird on his tongue, and while he wasn't sure he believed them, his bear had no doubts in his mind. "What happened?"

For a second, he didn't think she was going to answer him, but then she reached out and snagged the front of his jumper. "She shifted, and I need help finding her. Unfortunately, her mother isn't in a fit state to help and her uncle has disappeared."

He let her pull him inside and close the door behind him. "Which way was she headed?"

"She's ended up in the back garden somewhere. I can't use my animal to find her. What can you change into?"

The woman was blunt.

"Bear."

"Good, at least you can climb trees. Take off your clothes and meet me out the back."

Okay, that was a little too blunt. "You said she shifted?"

"Nothing wrong with your ears. Now hurry up. I don't want her to fly away."

She turned around and rushed down the hallway. She didn't even appear surprised that Ari had turned up. He quickly struggled to take off his clothes and left them on the banister. For a split second, he caught a familiar scent—not Rayna, something else—but he ignored it. It would have to wait.

The essence of his bear swept over him and brought him to his knees. Arms and legs elongated. Muscles enlarged all over his body, covered with fur. An impressive amount. His perspective shifted as he lumbered forward on all fours. A lot of scents hit him at once, a few he recognized and one was a weird blending of two. The sweet heat of Rayna mixed with something even more unique.

Ari made his way outside. His larger body made maneuvering out of the doorframe and the wooden doorframe cracked. If she noticed his awkwardness, Ruth didn't mention it. She looked up into the trees and at the field behind her house.

"Took you long enough."

He fought against the urge to growl at her. *Where is she?*

Ruth couldn't read his mind, but she was obviously thinking the same thing. "This is my fault. I should have known something like this could happen. Rayna's been accomplishing the impossible for years."

A million questions raced through his head, but with a distinctly non-human mouth, he couldn't put words to any of them. He let his animal guide their steps, as his connection with Rayna had clicked firmly into place. Ari had never experienced anything like it. There had been miles between them, but he'd sensed her pain and distress. He couldn't have stopped himself from rushing to her side even if he had wanted to.

Rayna was close. Every step he took into the garden and the field just beyond it made him even more sure. If she had flown, she had to be in one of the trees. The grass was soft and wet underneath his paws, and as he walked, the fur on the back of his neck stood on end. He ungracefully made his way through the gate and into the woods. Small, nocturnal animals scattered as he entered their domain. Bears weren't the stealthiest animals, but that was the least of his concerns. If he could sense her, she sensed him as well. He flicked his tongue out, tasting the chilly night air: *fear*. His mate was scared.

He discovered the tree she hid in and laid down, resting his massive head on his paws. Ruth must have figured out his plan because she didn't join him. Instead, the older shifter returned to the house. Ari continued to wait. He knew Rayna had never seen him in animal form, but there was every chance she recognized him. She was the prey to Ari's predator, but she had to know he didn't mean her any harm.

After a while, there was a noise just above him. He held himself completely still, not wanting to spook her. The noise was deliberate. She wasn't trying to mask the noises she made. It was hard to tell, but he needed to give her time. Ari couldn't remember the first time he shifted but Rayna had lived her whole life without thinking she could. Nerves were more than normal.

Trust me, love. I don't mean you any harm.

She had to recognize him. To know who he was with every ounce of her being because it was the only thing that made sense in a world where not many things made anything close to sense.

The movement continued above him. The bitter emotions were still there. The uncertainty. He had only the barest of warnings as twigs snapped above him and something feathery hit his back. He grunted but tried hard to keep himself completely still. The bird squawked and rolled off him in an ungraceful heap. Still, Ari didn't do anything other than turn his head to the side, taking in the sight of her. His chest went tight. How could she be so beautiful? Her shape reminded him of a peacock with the feathers draped across her body. Her neck was long, and a delicate curve led up to a sharp black beak. Caladrius.

What had happened to spark the shift?

Ari let his own shift sweep over him, enduring the sharp bite of pain as he became human again. When he was finished, he lay naked on the ground, the strands of grass tickling his private bits. The panic in her eyes eased toward relief. She'd have known who he was in his animal form, but it was new. At least his human face had some familiarity that could comfort her.

"Rayna, it's time for you to come back to me."

She tilted her head to the side then shook her head. There was every chance she didn't even know how. Ari moved into a more comfortable position, not bothered by his nakedness.

"Listen to me. I won't lie and say it won't hurt, but in the end, you won't remember it." He gingerly reached out and tickled the feathers at the top of her head. "You are stunning in this form, but I fell for the human first. Also, our human shapes are really compatible. I enjoy kissing that sweet mouth of yours. The beak will not make that easy, not even a little bit."

She tilted her head to the side again. Then she hunched over, the feathers disappearing. He wanted to pull her into his arms, to take the pain and discomfort away, but he couldn't. This was something she needed to experience.

In the end, she was breathless in front of him, her eyes shining and cheeks pink.

"I did it."

"I can see that."

It was obvious she was trying awfully hard to keep her eyes above his shoulders. "No, not that. I helped my mum."

"You healed her?"

She nodded, biting her bottom lip. "It means I can try to heal Daisy. I'm not a hundred percent sure how I did it." She glanced down at her naked body. Ari definitely liked what he saw. "I'm naked."

"Usually happens when you shift." He offered his hand, and when she touched it, he pulled her toward him. They collapsed to the ground. Rayna gasped in surprise but didn't pull away from him, and Ari laughed. All that worry about lying and manipulating her, and it hadn't mattered. Daisy was going to be healed, and he had found his mate.

You did lie to her though. She'll find out the truth.

Which means I'm going to have to be the one to tell her.

He pushed the thoughts to the back of his hand. She felt so good on top of him, and he held her close. "You seem very happy right now," she said.

Ari pushed his hips forward. "What gave me away?"

"Just something little."

He rolled her onto her back, positioning himself between her legs. "What do you mean, little?"

Her eyes darkened. "There's nothing little about you."

He pushed himself forward. "If we weren't in your grand-mother's garden…"

"What would you do?"

Acutely aware that they were near a house that belonged to shifters, Ari lowered his head, brushing his lips against the curve of her ear. "I would push myself into your wetness and fuck you till neither of us could think straight. Make you cry out my name over and over, until your voice becomes hoarse and you can't say anything else. Make sweat drip down the curves of your body, leaving your skin flushed and dewy." He pulled away, looking at her. "What do you think?"

"That I wish I wasn't lying naked in the grass of my grandmother's garden. How did you know something was wrong?"

"I just knew I needed to come to you." He brushed a kiss against her lips. "Come back with me?"

"To yours?"

"I don't want to spend the night without you. Please, Rayna." She moaned as he kissed her again, dipping his tongue between her lips. If they stayed this way for much longer, then grandmother be damned. He could feel Rayna's wetness, hot and welcoming. One flex of his hips and all control would be completely lost. "Will you come back with me?"

She nodded. "I'll check on Mum first and grab some clothes."

He reluctantly moved off her, and her gaze swept over him. She raised an eyebrow at the sight of him.

"Can you grab my trousers from inside on the banister? I'd rather not face your family with this." He gestured at his hard cock. "I'd rather not flash your nan if I can help it."

CHAPTER NINETEEN

Ruth greeted Rayna with an enormous hug. After accepting Ruth's congratulations on her shift—and being able to return to human form—Rayna checked in on Hiriko. Her mum had gone back to sleep, but Ruth gave her word that Hiriko was still lucid. They would know more in the morning, but all signs pointed to Hiriko being healed.

"It will still take time for her to work through her grief, but at least she's going to be able to," Ruth assured her.

"Should I stay?" Rayna asked, looking back at her sleeping mother.

"You mean stay here, or go to your mate's home?" Ruth asked with a raised eyebrow and a sly smile. "Don't you dare stay here. You have much to celebrate."

"What happened to Uncle Declan?" Rayna suddenly asked, wondering why he wasn't there congratulating her too.

"I have no idea. I'm as confused as you are as to why my son vanished when we needed him the most."

"He seemed perturbed earlier. It must really bother him to know that Dad's wreck wasn't an accident."

"Don't worry about me or Declan," Ruth said, ushering her down the stairs. "Focus on your mate and all the possibilities the future now holds for you. Rayna, now that you have an animal, you're eligible for FUC agent training."

"Unless ASS demands I go with them." The Avian Soaring Society liked to train their own and would want the opportunity to brag about having a caladrius in their ranks.

"Worry about that later. For now, pack an overnight bag and go to your bear."

<hr />

RAYNA HAD CURLED UP IN THE PASSENGER SIDE, WATCHING ARI as he drove. She still couldn't believe what had happened. Being with Ari and sharing a few kisses had started her transformation until nothing could have brought it to a halt.

Her mate.

The speed of things made her head spin. Her father's death had brought her home into the path of her mate. Without it, she wouldn't have met him. Never known he existed. The thought filled her with sadness. She still would have wished her father in her life.

She reached out and touched his arm.

He glanced down at her, his expression soft. "What?"

"Have you found out anything about my dad?"

He frowned slightly. "I put a couple of feelers out. I imagine I might hear back at some point tomorrow." He pulled into his parking spot, and instead of getting out of the car, Rayna climbed into his lap. "Don't want to wait?"

"We're at your home. There's no light around us. You don't have any neighbors."

"Sounds like you've put some thought into this."

"You promised me a lot of things, and I'd rather not run the risk of waking your daughter."

"This won't be comfortable."

Rayna took his hand as he spoke and guided it between her legs.

"You're not wearing underwear. Fuck, you're wet."

Rayna shuddered as he pushed a finger inside of her, and she grabbed his shoulders. Her whole body had been in a heightened state of awareness since she shifted. She needed him in a way she had never needed anyone before.

"I want you, Ari. I don't want to wait any longer."

"Goddess, I love it when you call me that." He continued to move his fingers in and out of her. "I'll give you what you need, but our first time won't be in my car. I have a guest cottage at the back of the house."

She thought he was going to pully away from her, but he kissed her instead. One hand remained between her thighs, teasing her to heights she'd never experienced before. The other hand cradled her face. She rode his fingers until she came to a shuddering climax. He broke his sweet contact with her lips, and she asked, "How far away is the guesthouse?"

"Not far away at all." He opened his door, and Rayna scooted out. Then he followed her. It was impossible to miss the hard rigid bulge just under his trousers. "Around the corner, at the end of the garden. The lights will be off, but you won't miss it."

"Aren't you coming with me?"

His smile looked positively wicked. "I'm going to count to five, and then I'm going to chase you."

That sounded ridiculously hot. Rayna didn't question him, and as soon as he started counting, she ran. It felt like a monster was chasing her, ready to rip off her clothes and devour her. The thought should have scared her, but it didn't. She could still feel the ghost of his fingers between her legs, and the orgasm had left her legs weak. Was it her more animalistic urges that made her this way? Another thing she had never experienced, or it could have been something else.

Mate.

She made her way around the corner, kicking off her shoes—which ended up in a hedge—and continued to run. She would have loved more time to explore the garden. Hendrickson had a skill that surprised her. The bear shifter had created something beautiful.

The lower part of the guesthouse was mostly made up of glass-like panels. She pulled open the door. Her heartbeat was impossibly loud in her ears. It had nothing to do with fear and everything to do with desire.

Rayna wanted him to catch her.

She slid the door closed and backed away from the door. A hand clamped over her mouth. She squeaked before Ari's scent enveloped her.

"Did you really think you could beat me, little bird?"

She shook her head. Desire pooled between her legs, and he reached to the front of her dress. There was no warning as he tore the dress to ribbons. By the time he was finished, Rayna stood naked and completely at his mercy.

He stepped in front of her. The look in his eyes was dark and unreadable. He raised his fingers to his lips and licked them. Rayna couldn't look away. "I knew you were going to taste sweet."

He took a step toward her, and she took a step back. There weren't any lights, so they moved in near darkness.

"Do you still want all the things I promised you?"

The atmosphere between them had changed. The thing that tied them together was deeper than anything she had experienced before. The man who stalked her was her mate. The way he had handled her, taking control of the situation, was enough to clear her mind of any doubts. Ari wouldn't hurt her.

The backs of her knees hit something, a chair. Ari placed a hand on her bare shoulder and guided her down. The wood was cool against her bottom. "You can use your words, little bird. Tell me you still want this. Tell me you still want me."

They were questions, but she found herself looking up, meeting his gaze. "I still want this."

The corner of his lips twitched like he was suppressing a smile. "Then I want another taste." He dropped to his knees. He picked her feet up, positioning them on his shoulders. Rayna felt exposed, and she was suddenly glad for the darkness. That didn't mean much to people with night vision, but she didn't focus on that. She bit her lip as he trailed kisses up her thighs. She rolled her head back, closing her eyes and letting herself drown in the sensations. Her animal delighted in the contact with her mate. A gasp escaped her as he nibbled, licked, and teased.

"Ari…"

He dug his fingertips into her thighs, feasting on her. She would have bruises in the morning, but she didn't care. Rayna wanted his mark on her, even with a healing ability that would erase any damage he did. Her next orgasm building at a steady pace, she grabbed the armrests, and everything went white. Even as the afterglow faded, he continued to lick her clean. She tried to get her breathing under control, but the teasing was relentless, and she felt herself caught up in another one, just as intense as the last.

Rayna collapsed against the chair, and Ari looked up the line of her body, a smirk on his face. He knew exactly the effect he'd had on her. There was no shame in those dark eyes.

"I would ask if you liked that, but I can still taste the evidence of your release on my tongue."

Her face burned hot. There was no way he could miss it, and he chuckled. Then he offered his hand. "How about I show you the rest of the guesthouse."

CHAPTER TWENTY

FOR THE FIRST TIME IN FOREVER, ARI AVERUS WAS HAPPY. THE Goddess had blessed him with a powerful mate. Sure, there were complications, but she would be able to save his daughter. That was all that mattered. He led her by the hand to the guesthouse bedroom. She didn't hide her nakedness, but after what they had done and shared with each other, there was nothing left to hide.

Except you're the Broker. What is she going to do when she finds out the truth?

Ari pushed the thought to the back of his mind. That was a question for tomorrow. Tonight, he planned on focusing on her. For one night the world didn't exist outside the four walls of the guesthouse. In the morning, she would heal his daughter, and then he would tell her who he truly was. She deserved to hear it from him. The trust she placed in him was intoxicating.

The housekeepers kept the guesthouse clean of dust. Ari didn't like to entertain guests, but the house had come with the building. He pushed the bedroom door open and motioned for her to enter before him. She glanced up at him, goosebumps across her naked flesh, and then stepped into the bedroom.

"Can I help with that?" She gestured to the bulge barely contained by his trousers.

Ari wanted to get her onto the bed, to bury his cock in her warm heat. The thought of her on her knees, his cock between her lips, made him uncomfortably hard. She sounded so innocent, even with the way she had saddled him in his car. There had been a flash of worry.

A thought crept into his head and took root. "Rayna, are you a virgin?"

Her blush deepened. "I've done stuff before, but yes." She knelt in front of him, all dark eyes, with the distinctive white streak in her hair. She reached for the belt on his trousers, and he watched as she unbuckled it. "I want to do this with you. Please, Ari." The piece of leather hit the ground.

He reached down to cup her face. "Since you asked so nicely." His words could have sounded smug, even a little cocky, but a warmth spread over him. Her desire was a thing of beauty. Even her inexperience did funny things to him.

She pulled his trousers down, and he groaned as she nudged the hard rigid flesh. The move was almost animalistic, instinctive. With the wall behind him, he was trapped, but he could get away if he wanted. He waited for her to get comfortable, and then she freed him completely. Her eyes widened slightly. Ari was larger than average, and he could understand if the sight and feel of his cock was a little intimidating.

"We'll take it slow," he promised her. Ari was going to lose his mind if she kept looking at him like that. As soon as she took him into her warm, wet mouth, it was going to be a fight for control. He wasn't going to embarrass himself.

She nodded and then touched him.

"Feel it, run your hand up and down its silky length," he

growled as she followed his instructions. He already started leaking pre-cum, leaving the head shiny and sensitive.

She edged forward, the tip of her tongue out, and tasted him. Ari closed his eyes. If he watched her take him, he wouldn't have lasted longer than a minute. The briefest look he'd allowed himself had been sexy as hell. He had no clue what to do with his hands, so he laced his fingers into the heavy strands of her hair. He didn't want to take control. He wanted her to have the opportunity to explore at her own pace.

Then she took more of him into his mouth.

"Holy fuck." He strained, fighting against the urge to get her to take more of him, to fill up her mouth.

"Is this okay?"

"It's perfect, Rayna. You're perfect."

She went back to working his hard rigid length, and the pressure built in the pit of his stomach. Then she did something different, a swirl of her tongue, like his cock was the world's best ice cream. That one move left him seeing stars, and he knew he couldn't wait any longer.

He pulled her up by her shoulders and crashed his lips against hers. They did a weird dance as they moved to the bed, toppling onto the sheets together. They were both breathing heavily, and he continued to kiss her as he reached between her legs. The top of her thighs were wet from her arousal. She felt more than ready for him.

He pushed a finger inside of her then another. She cried out, the sound a mixture of pleasure and pain.

"I need to make sure you're ready for me. I don't want to hurt you."

"You won't."

She grabbed him again, sitting up to meet him, but he pushed her down. "Spread your legs for me."

A blush crept over her face and down her chest. She looked away as she reached down and did what he asked.

"Never be embarrassed by your body."

"A little hard not to be when you're looking at me like that."

He lay down between her thighs. "I want every inch of this body. The look in my eyes is pure need." He traced a path along the lips, stopping as he reached the cluster of hooded nerves. He slipped one finger inside of her, working it in and out. As he did, he started to feast. It didn't take long for her to become a quivering mess, chanting his name as she rolled her hips, fucking his finger. Then he added another finger, doing a come-hither motion against her G-spot. The scream that ripped through the quiet guest home made him happy they had ended up here and not in his bedroom.

Her arousal coated his mouth, and she slumped against the bed, boneless. Ari allowed himself a smile as he crawled up her body, placing kisses on her nipples and neck. "Enjoy that?"

She nodded, slightly dazed.

He hooked one of her legs over his arm. His cock was impossibly hard and nudged against her wet slit. Slowly he pushed inside of her, and the dazed look vanished, replaced with heat. "Look at how beautifully you take me, little bird." Her gaze flickered down, and she bit her lip.

"More."

He pushed another inch inside of her. There was a little resistance, and he lowered himself, half covering her body with his. "This might hurt. If you want me to stop, say so." He didn't know where he would find the strength, but he would. Hurting her was the furthest thing from his mind. "Promise me."

"I promise."

The words were barely out of her mouth when Ari did

two things at once. He thrust inside of her and bit her earlobe. The idea was simply to overload her with sensations so she couldn't focus on just one thing. For a second, he didn't move, letting her grow accustomed to his length. She was practically shaking in his arms.

"Are you okay?"

"That hurt." Her eyes were wide and her breathing shallow.

"Do you want me to stop?" He really didn't want to stop but he would if she asked.

"No, it just took me by surprise."

He started to move, pinning her hands above her head, and he thrust inside of her. It was a loose hold. If she wanted to escape, she could, but he got the distinct impression she liked when he took control. The things he could teach her. He buried his head against the curve of her throat, breathing in her scent, marveling at the way her wetness encased him. She moaned beneath him; her breathing picked up the pace. There was a rise to her hips, meeting each of his thrusts, allowing him to go deeper, a little harder.

Fuck, he was going to lose his mind.

"This feels really good."

"I aim to please."

The mattress was soft beneath them. The covers around them a tangled mess. She was going to come again. Her pussy clutched him tight like a fist, and he groaned. Being with her was pure madness, but he didn't care. He wanted all of her. To feel her come again would be the ultimate reward. A sign he had done his job right. They would worry about tomorrow when it got here.

He brushed his lips against her ear. "You're going to be a good girl, aren't you?"

She nodded. Her skin flushed, and her black eyes told him more than words ever could.

"Then come for me, little bird. Come for me." He growled those last words. That was all she needed. She strained against his hold, and he let her free. The position was still perfect, and as she screamed his name, he followed her into the abyss.

Perfection.

CHAPTER TWENTY-ONE

Rayna barely remembered the night before. As she woke up, it was a wild flash of images. Shifting for the first time. Not into the seal that would have meant she had inherited that part from her father. No, she was a bird shifter like her mum. She had healed Hiriko before she shifted for the first time, completely overwhelmed by her animal. At the moment, the caladrius was blissfully quiet. Rayna knew the reason behind it.

She turned on her side and looked at the man next to her. Ari Averus. Bear shifter and her mate. Everything had happened so fast it had left her head spinning.

She took her time studying his profile. Morning light came in through the netted curtains, highlighting a strong jaw and a nose that had a slight bump at the bridge. Full lips, his mouth slightly open as he slept. The things they had done last night. Rayna had gone from virgin to experiencing heady heights. Her body was still sore, but there was no real damage, even if she felt a little shell-shocked.

Rayna left the bed, retrieving Ari's shirt off the floor and slipping it on. The pure animalistic scent of a predator made her stomach tight with need again.

Predator and prey. They shouldn't have been mates, but it wasn't uncommon.

She went in search of a bathroom and freshened up. At some point last night her hairband had snapped, leaving her hair down around her shoulders. She ran her fingers through it to work out the tangles and then splashed some water on her face.

When she returned to the bed, she found Ari was still asleep, and she crawled in next to him. She didn't have long before she needed to return to Ruth's and see her mum. She still couldn't believe that her caladrius had managed to reach her, and while that made her feel elated, she was brought down by the fact that her father was still gone. Hiriko was going to have to face it, just like Rayna and Ruth did.

She could just imagine how happy he'd be for her, knowing she could shift now. And she knew he would have been incredibly proud of her for healing her mum.

But they weren't the only family with misfortunes. She couldn't forget about Daisy. Would she be able to heal Daisy?

"You're thinking very hard."

Ari's voice jolted her back to the present. "I thought you were still asleep."

"I'm a light sleeper. What's on your mind?"

"You really want to know?"

"I wouldn't have asked if I didn't."

She looked up at the ceiling. She still wore his shirt, and his scent calmed the animal inside of her. It also did an excellent job calming her human nerves. "When do you want to see if I can help Daisy?"

He stilled next to her. He had to have been thinking the same thing but was too polite to push the issue.

"The problem with Daisy is on a genetic level. I don't know if your ability will work."

"It won't hurt to give it a try."

"That's true. How are you feeling?" He rolled onto his side, his hand propping up his head, and he looked down at her.

"A little sore," she said honestly. "But I assume that's normal." She gingerly reached up and touched her ear, which didn't hurt anymore. "Why did you bite me?"

"As a distraction. You were a virgin, and I don't mean to boast, but I'm slightly bigger than average."

She giggled, and his gaze narrowed. Suddenly she was pinned underneath him again. The move was so quick it barely registered. His cock was hard again, heavy against her thigh.

"You don't think I am?"

"I really don't have anything to compare it to. It's pretty big, but what makes it big? All I have is your word." She licked her lips. "We could always test it out again."

"Very tempting, little bird."

She raised herself up onto her elbows, bringing her face close to his. She liked seeing him this way, relaxed and happy. There was still some darkness in his gaze, worry about his daughter and something else. Rayna had gotten good at reading people in her FUC training, but it had been like seeing things in black and white. Now everything was in color. It was amazing. She closed the distance between them and kissed him.

He pulled away slightly. "Let's go see Daisy. She really wanted to meet you."

A warm feeling spread in her chest. "You told her about me?"

The corner of his mouth twitched. "I might have mentioned you. Is that okay?"

Rayna knew they were a package deal. Ari was her mate, and Daisy was an important part of his life. Which meant the little girl would have to become an important part of Rayna's life. She was more than okay with that. "I haven't got a problem with that."

Ari ran to the car to retrieve her overnight bag she'd forgotten the night before. He returned, and after they got dressed, he made a phone call just outside the front door. She was tempted to listen in but stopped herself short of giving in to the temptation. If it involved her father's murder, she was sure he would mention it.

I'm going to find out what happened to you, Dad. I promise.

"Are you ready to meet her?"

She glanced up to see Ari had opened the door, sending in a blast of chilly morning air. She nodded as she took his offered hand. "Let's go see if I can help her."

A CALMNESS SWEPT OVER RAYNA WHENEVER ARI TOUCHED HER. It helped to ease her racing heart. She really wanted to talk to someone about the connection between mates, but it felt wrong to discuss it with her grandmother or mother, who'd both lost theirs. Maybe there was someone at the Academy. Perhaps Aubrey, the librarian, since she had a mate. Even Suzanna, her dorm mate, while not mated, still might know more than Rayna did. She had no idea if it was normal to feel this way.

They walked to the main house and to the kitchen. Soft sounds came from behind the closed door.

Through the glass she spotted Hendrickson in front of the oven, an apron around his waist. She smiled to herself, realizing the man was more than a driver and gardener.

Behind him, Daisy sat at the table. The little girl's face was pale, and there were dark circles beneath her eyes.

There was no point in denying, even just to herself, that she had butterflies in the pit of her stomach. A lot rested on whether or not she could heal Daisy. What if it was a one-time thing? What if the effort of healing took too much from her and she couldn't do it again? She'd been so drained after she healed her mum, before her body had been taken over by the shift.

Her mum had discussed the powers of the caladrius with her often when she was younger, and everyone had thought she'd shift at sixteen, but Rayna now realized that she hadn't learned enough. She knew that the caladrius had become a bird of myth because the lineage of people with the ability to shift into the bird was so small. She also knew that the myth said the bird shifter touched the body of the one who needed their aid, took their illness, and flew away, taking the illness with them.

It was a beautiful myth, if not completely accurate. The caladrius shifters didn't need to fly away each time. Of course, Rayna had done exactly that the night before, so who knew how it worked for her?

They entered the kitchen, and Daisy looked at them, her face lighting up. "Are you Ray-Ray?"

Rayna smiled at the little girl. "That's me, and you must be Daisy. You're just as beautiful as your dad said you are."

Her cheeks turned a light shade of pink.

"What do we say to someone who pays us a compliment, sweet pea?" Ari chimed in.

"Thank you."

"You're more than welcome. What are you eating for breakfast?" Rayna approached the table, eying the plates. She was starving.

"Henny is making pancakes."

Rayna shot a smile toward the bear shifter, who had his back to her. His shoulders were tense. "They smell delicious, Henny."

"Only Daisy can call me that," the man replied quickly. He started to serve up the food. Despite the gruffness, he still offered, "I can make something else if you like."

The little girl watched her, and Rayna got the distinct impression it was a test of sorts. Rayna pulled out a chair at the table. "Do you have chocolate spread?"

"Of course. Those are Daisy's favorite."

"Then, absolutely. That's the only way to have pancakes." Daisy smiled. Rayna had passed the test.

During the whole interaction, Ari had been quiet. She noted that he had been since he'd taken that phone call. Whatever the conversation had been about weighed heavily on his mind. Either that or he was worried about what would happen next. There was a lot that rested on his shoulders.

He sat down on the other side of the table, on Daisy's right side. Hendrickson dished out the pancakes and then sat opposite Daisy, eating his own stack. Rayna helped Daisy spread out the chocolate on her pancakes, noting the bandage on her arm, covering the crux of her elbow.

"Did you stay here last night?"

At the little girl's question, Rayna nearly choked on her pancakes and Ari coughed like his own breakfast had gotten lodged in his throat. What on earth was she supposed to say to that?

"She did. She was pretty tired last night, so she slept in the guesthouse." Ari shot Rayna a heated look, and she tried hard to stop blushing.

They hadn't discussed how they were going to do this. Did Ari expect Rayna to take Daisy's hand and see if her ability to heal took over? Her animal had been quiet since she woke up. Was she too tired to heal Daisy?

"How about after breakfast you show Ray-Ray your room?"

"You're not going to come with us?"

He shook his head. "I need to talk to Henny about some boring adult stuff. I'll join you when I finish up."

The faintest trace of a lie, close enough to the truth that if Rayna hadn't been looking for it, she wouldn't have sensed it.

"You can see my collection of teddies. Whenever dad travels, he always brings me back one."

"Do you have a favorite?"

Daisy moved a teddy bear off her lap and handed it to Rayna. A rich brown color and button eyes. "What's his name?"

"Daddy. You can hold on to Daddy if you want. Feel his ears. They're so soft."

Now Rayna couldn't stop the blush that made her face go hot. Ari still watched her, and she could feel the weight in his gaze. "He's adorable. I can see why he's your favorite."

CHAPTER TWENTY-TWO

Ari watched as the pair walked out of the kitchen. The sight did funny things to his heart, and a warmth spread through him. His daughter and his mate. It finally felt like his world was clicking into place. There were only a few things he had to get out of the way.

Hendrickson had moved to the sink and had started to wash the dishes. Ari made his way to the coffee machine.

"I see she spent the night."

"She shifted last night. After she healed her mum."

A glass broke, and the water in the sink turned red. Hendrickson pulled out his hands, and the cuts healed. "Are you sure?"

"I saw her in her bird form. She was magnificent. I've never seen anything like her before."

The larger man picked up the kitchen towel and dried his hands. Usually, he was impossible to read, even for Ari's bear. But at that moment Ari could read him like an open book. His friend smiled. Something he only ever did when he was with Daisy.

"When is she going to heal her?"

"Soon. It isn't an exact science, but we know it's possible." He felt positively peaceful when he had woken that morning with Rayna in his arms. There was only one way it could have been better. "Rayna asked me to look into her dad's murder."

Hendrickson frowned. "You sure it was murder and not an accident? Those roads can be dangerous for those who aren't used to them."

"Yes. Her grandmother's intel revealed the brake lines were cut. On top of that, Kya got back in contact with me this morning."

"I thought she was supposed to be returning to the house. I was wondering what was taking her so long."

"She's been caught up digging into our mysterious Mr. Black." The fox shifter didn't like mysteries, and she certainly didn't like the idea of someone manipulating them to their own ends. It was a different story when the manipulation was their own doing.

"The man who came to you with the information about Rayna?"

Ari nodded. "I think Adam Jensen was still alive when Mr. Black visited me. I already thought the timing was off and he was sketchy as hell. Which means the only way he could have gotten that information to me so fast…"

"If he was somehow involved."

"Exactly." Ari leaned against the counter. "I don't think he was the one to cut the brake lines himself, but it seems likely he hired someone or is working with someone else. That he concocted a scheme that involved murdering Adam Jensen to awaken Rayna's caladrius *and* bring her back to the UK…"

"But her caladrius didn't awaken when her father died," Hendrickson pointed out.

"Mr. Black took a risk, and it didn't pan out, but it looks like meeting me did awaken the caladrius."

"So, Adam Jensen died for no reason."

Ari shook his head sadly. "I hope this isn't the case. I hope there's some other explanation, but the only one we have isn't much better. That being that Rayna's grandparents, the Aikawas, were behind it. Getting revenge on Adam for taking their daughter away from them so many years ago."

"That's a lot of years to wait for revenge." Hendrickson was a great believer in family. The ones you were born into and the ones you were unofficially adopted into. He couldn't get his head around betraying family. "So, Kaya finally found something on Black?"

Ari took a deep breath, reluctant to admit what they'd learned. "Information on him has been hard to come by. And we knew that if Kya had a problem finding it, it meant someone really wanted to keep the information buried."

"To what end?"

"So they can get paid a hell of a lot of money from me—someone in dire need of a powerful healer—without anyone learning what they did. He might have thought it was a price worth paying. People do a lot of shitty things for money."

None of Ari's clients were innocent people. Their motives were always murky. Ari had never judged any of them because they paid him a lot of money. Sometimes he thought he was no better than them. Even if his intentions were pure. Everyone was the hero in their own stories. Ari knew there were people out there, especially in FUC, who wouldn't believe that. Rayna might not. He dreaded telling her the truth. For a few moments, he wanted to believe everything would be okay, that she would be able to heal his daughter and they could talk about their future together.

"I can see why anyone would want to avoid starting a war with the Redfield seal pod, but the way you're talking makes it sound like it's more personal than that. Who's Mr. Black?"

"Declan Jensen."

"Her uncle?"

"Yes." Ari slumped his shoulders. "I thought I recognized the scent when I entered Ruth's home. I was just too preoccupied with helping Rayna to put two and two together."

"Adam Jensen's brother was behind his death?" Hendrickson looked horrified. "And you haven't told Rayna, have you?"

"I haven't had time to figure out how to do that. The family grieving one brother, just to have everything torn apart again when they learn what the other brother did? And then we have to consider that Declan knows I'm the Broker. There's a risk of all of this blowing up in our faces."

"Then maybe you need to tell Rayna the truth. About Declan and yourself. It'll be best if it comes from you."

Ari rubbed his mouth. Hendrickson was right. "Let's see if she can heal Daisy first. My little girl can't wait any longer. Then I'll tell Rayna everything."

"What do you need me to do?"

"Find out where Declan is, and we'll figure out what to do next. Rayna and her family deserve justice. Just don't spook him. He has a lot of money, and he might try to run if he thinks he's in danger." Ari finished his drink and put the cup in the sink. "I'm going to find my girls."

"You say that like Rayna is a part of this family."

That warm feeling in his chest hadn't gone anywhere. "She is. Henny, she's my mate."

"Are you sure?"

"There's no question in my mind. My bear recognizes her, and she feels the same way."

Ari found them in Daisy's room. Rayna must have lifted her onto the hospital bed, and Daisy had scattered the teddy bears between them. He leaned in the doorway and watched the pair of them talk. The little girl spoke with a maturity well past her age, even when it was about teddy bears. It was because Daisy didn't have friends her own age. Hendrickson was like an uncle, and Kya was a fun aunt, but in her state, she had been unable to go out and socialize with kids her own age. It was just too risky. Being sheltered might have meant her withdrawing into herself, but she had never been that way. She had a confidence, a light that was uniquely hers.

Now he couldn't help but see possibilities. If Rayna healed Daisy, then Daisy could go to school. Finally make friends and be around her peers. Then there was the possibility that he and Rayna could bring new children into the family. Give Daisy the little brother or sister she'd always wanted.

The idea warmed him.

"So, what's this one called?"

"Happy. I called these ones after the Seven Dwarfs."

Rayna sat on the end of the bed, her legs crossed. She listened with an intent focus, nodding and asking questions. Neither of them had looked in his direction, but Rayna must have sensed him.

"What do you do for fun?"

"I talk to my bears. Henny reads to me."

"What's your favorite story?"

"'Snow White and the Three Bears.'"

"That's a happy story." Rayna didn't correct the title but kept the conversation moving forward. "Do you go outside in Henny's beautiful gardens?"

Daisy shook her head. "Not really. Daddy doesn't talk much about it, but I know I'm sick." She hugged her favorite teddy to her chest. "He's tried a lot to make me better."

"He's still trying."

"I know." Daisy yawned.

Rayna offered her hands to Daisy, who crawled into her lap with a level of trust that amazed him. He stepped into her bedroom and makeshift hospital room. Rayna glanced in his direction but turned her attention immediately back to Daisy. She held both of the girl's little hands and closed her eyes. Ari sat in the place Daisy had just vacated. He had only felt so completely helpless once, and it wasn't a feeling he enjoyed.

The energy in the room shifted. Rayna's animal danced to the surface, summoned by the pain of the girl in Rayna's arms. Though Rayna stayed in her human form, ghost-like wings spread from her back, feathered like a bird. The change was almost ethereal, angelic.

He didn't know what to say, if he should say anything at all. All he could remember was what happened following the last time. The way he had found her hidden up the trees, terrified. Rayna hadn't mastered her abilities. She was being brave for Daisy, but she was scared. Ari's bear could sense it, and instinctively Ari reached out, resting his hand on her knee, willing his strength to her. Mates shared a connection. Ari had always thought it was a myth. He'd thought that the connection he shared with Becca had been enough, but with Rayna, it was completely different. He was whole, and even as the thought crept into his head, he pushed it away. He didn't regret his time with his wife. If he hadn't fallen in love with the rabbit, he never would have had Daisy. A life without his daughter wasn't a life he wanted to be a part of.

Which was why this had to work. It was his last hope. Daisy was out of time.

"I'm here."

His daughter's eyes flickered open, and she smiled. "Hey, Daddy."

Beads of sweat appeared on Rayna's forehead, and the

previously serene expression on her face became strained. He squeezed her knee, and her eyes opened. The irises and pupils had been drowned out by pure white. "Take her, Ari." She squeezed the words out.

He collected Daisy from Rayna's arms, and Rayna fell off the bed. By the time she hit the floor, her human form was gone and a bird was in her place among her discarded clothes.

Daisy's eyes went impossibly wide as she looked up at him. "Is that Ray-Ray?" He nodded. "She's beautiful."

The caladrius strutted over to the window and nudged the latch with her beak.

"Rayna, stay with us." Ari spoke sternly, not wanting her to flee in fear and panic as she had the night before.

But the bird swiveled her head toward him, and suddenly he understood. The caladrius of myth needed to carry the illness far away from the inflicted. She needed to go outside to complete the ritual.

Ari carried Daisy to the window, opening it for Rayna. He had to take a step back as she spread her wings and managed to hop onto the windowsill.

"Thank you," Ari mouthed.

She nodded, the move incredibly human in a body that wasn't. Then she took off into the sky.

Ari let his bear come to the surface and sniff Daisy, who had fallen asleep in his arms. He noticed the change immediately. Previously Daisy had something bitter in her aura. Something unmistakable, unique to her and a constant reminder she was destined for an early death.

Now? Freshly cut grass. Summers as it turned to winter. *Health and happiness.* His bear recognized something else. A presence inside of her. A small animal had woken up. It was too early to know if she carried a bear or rabbit, but something eased in his chest. His eyes burned, and it took a moment for him to feel the tears roll down his face. The last time he had cried was when he begged for Becca's life. Anger at his own perceived weakness. He had been trained to save lives, and he had failed her.

Daisy's going to be okay.

He embraced the dangerous emotion that settled in the pit of his stomach. Hope.

Everything's going to be okay.

He looked out of the window. Rayna was out of sight, but he had no doubt she would return to them. He owed her a price that could never be repaid, and now he could only hope she would forgive him for the part he'd played in the greatest tragedy of her life.

CHAPTER TWENTY-THREE

Rayna had lost consciousness when she shifted for the first time. She had blacked out, with no idea what had happened between healing her mum and ending up in the tree. Her animal had operated on instinct, but now, Rayna was learning in leaps and bounds. The years that had been lost to her had hit her with a speed that took her breath away. It was insanity. Her whole life had changed in the blink of an eye. One moment she had resigned herself to a mundane life, working as a civilian contact for FUC and watching a world she sat apart from. That was no longer the case.

When she healed Daisy, a heavy weight settled in the pit of her stomach. She didn't know what it meant, but she remembered the myths and legends of her people. She flew into the sky, away from Ari's home. Something instinctual guided her, but Rayna didn't question it. She kept above the clouds. Far enough away from human eyes. Unless she was really unlucky and she was seen by a plane. There was no way she would be mistaken for a normal bird. Her white feathers were camouflaged against the clouds, which meant nobody should see her if they took that moment to look up at the sky.

There were a lot of questions brewing inside of her. A lot of things she wanted answers to. She planned on having a lot of conversations with her mum. Hiriko Jensen was going to be okay. The pain of losing her mate would prey heavily on her heart, but she was no longer trapped in the confines of her mind. Rayna trusted that Declan and Ruth would look after her once Rayna returned to the Academy.

She still couldn't believe that she'd be going back with a shifter side. That she'd actually be allowed to start traditional agent training.

She understood why Ruth didn't want to bring the FUC into their personal matters. It wasn't that she had anything against agents. It was just that involving the agency would take Adam's case out of their control. Rayna had to trust Ari would be able to figure out who was behind it.

Rayna flapped her wings, soaring over the clouds, higher and higher before curving and diving, bursting free of the cloudbank. For the first time in her life, Rayna was free. There was no judgment up in the sky. Her animal was in control, and Rayna watched the world go by.

After a while, the pressure in her stomach eased and a lightness swept over her. She made her way back to Ari's house—it was easy to pick out the vivid colors of the flowers and the guesthouse. She spied him in the back garden, sitting next to a small table. With her animal in control, her eyesight was amazing. Rayna could make out every detail of his handsome face, even the dark shade of his eyes as he looked up at her. As she landed, she noted the chair next to him, which had clothes folded on top of it. On the table were two cups of something hot and steaming and... cake?

The shift back into her human form was strange. From human to bird hadn't been too bad, but suddenly there was a tremendous pressure all over her body. Feathers vanished back inside her body That was a strange sensation. When it was finally over, she got to her feet, feeling vulnerable. Ari approached her with a rich purple robe in his hands. He draped the satiny fabric over her shoulders.

When she was covered, he belted it in place and brushed a sweet but brief kiss against her lips. Her stomach tightened in need.

"How's she doing?"

"Sleeping, but I noticed that her scent has changed. You did it, Rayna." He didn't look happy, and she sensed an inner turmoil inside of him. She touched his chest, feeling the beat of his heart.

"What's wrong?"

"Let's sit down. Henny baked a cake yesterday and wanted for you to try a slice."

It didn't escape her notice that he hadn't answered her question. She sat down and peered into her cup. "What's this?" She breathed in the heavenly scent but couldn't place any of the ingredients.

"I called Ruth and told her what happened. She suggested this blend of ingredients to help center you."

"Did she mention my mum?"

"Ruth said that she's still resting but she's out of the woods."

"That's really good news." She took a sip of her drink, and some of the tension left her. "I really didn't think I could do it. If Ruth hadn't suggested trying to talk to her, I never would have reached her..." She found she couldn't finish the sentence. They wouldn't be celebrating, Daisy wouldn't have been healed, and her mum would have starved, dying from a broken heart.

"I knew you could do it."

"You did?"

"You can't see how strong you are. You've endured so much to reach this point. You're incredible."

Even as he said the sweetest words Rayna had ever heard, he didn't look at her. Rayna doubted the grass was worth that much attention. He kept something from her, but what? Was he worried about her returning to the Academy? They hadn't solved her dad's death, and she didn't plan to leave until they had answers. Neither of them had really talked about the future. It wouldn't be easy. Rayna was going to be an agent, and Ari's life was in Orchard with his daughter. Even if they were mates, there was a time limit. One that weighed heavily on her.

"Is something wrong?"

Ari glanced across at her, and she read the uncertainty in his eyes. He turned his attention back to the cup in his hands. "I have to tell you something."

"You know you can tell me anything." Rayna put her cup down and pulled her legs up, hugging them. Whatever was about to happen next, she wanted to be prepared. Hugging herself brought her a little bit of comfort.

For a moment they sat in silence, but he held himself still, like he didn't trust himself to move. She could read him on a level she hadn't been able to before. Was that a perk of being a shifter or because they were mates? It suddenly dawned on her that they hadn't had the conversation. She knew with every inch of her being that the man next to her was her mate. She thought he knew it too.

"I have to tell you something."

"You already said that."

He smiled, but there was no light, just a sadness. "I don't know how you'll react. You know I never used to be this way. Sure, I cared about people, but after Becca's death, I cared less. I didn't worry about hurting people's feelings. You changed that. I don't want to hurt you."

"You're scaring me, Ari."

"I don't mean to." He turned his attention back to the contents of his cup. "I know who was behind your dad's death."

Rayna froze. Of all the things he could have said, he told her that. Why would he worry about her reaction? She had gone to him for help. Why wouldn't she want to know the truth? Unless it had something to do with her mum's parents? That would destroy her mum all over again. Rayna had only just managed to get her back. "Are you sure?"

"A hundred percent. The call I took this morning was a contact, and they confirmed it."

Rayna frowned. There was a bitter smell. A faint trace of a lie, but which part was the lie? "Okay, who is it?"

He put his cup on the ground at his feet. He turned to face her. It looked like he wanted to reach out to her, but she didn't move to take his hand. "Declan Jensen."

She frowned. Had she misheard him? There had to be more than one Declan Jensen in the world. It couldn't be her uncle. What would he have to gain? What was his motive? "You're wrong."

His eyes filled with a sympathetic look. "I'm a lot of things, Rayna, but I'm not wrong. Not about this."

"Are you sure?"

"I've made it my job to be sure."

"You run a charity, Ari. You've asked sources you haven't been in contact with for years. It's not enough."

"It was enough when you wanted my help."

"You can't tell me my uncle is a murderer with no proof. They were brothers. He loved Dad." Her voice had started to quiver. She got to her feet, and Ari followed her.

"I'm not lying to you. What would *I* have to gain by wanting you to believe your uncle was behind your dad's death?"

Rayna couldn't think straight. It was all too much with everything else going on. Suddenly she got lightheaded.

He's not lying. You know he's not.

She grabbed the sides of her head. *Too much.*

Suddenly Ari reached for her. The touch broke through her confusion, centering her. For the briefest moment, she couldn't look away from him. Her animal wanted nothing more than to step into his embrace, to be held and comforted by him. She had trusted him to keep her safe.

"Head home. Talk to him. I wouldn't suggest telling him what I said, but you can shift now. You're a trainee agent, and you can detect lies. Go and talk to him, but don't confront him, Rayna. If I'm right, he's dangerous. We don't know what he's capable of."

CHAPTER TWENTY-FOUR

They drove in silence. Ari had to be wrong. Declan might have been the free-spirited uncle, but he wasn't a bad man. He brought her noisy toys to annoy her parents at Christmas. He told her brilliant stories about his adventures around the world. How could Ari think Declan was capable of murdering his own brother?

Ari parked, and Rayna looked at Ruth's home. There was no telling if Declan was in there. He might have gone out for the day, and it wasn't like Rayna could tell anyone else about Ari's concerns. It wasn't fair to even bring it up when it couldn't be true.

"Are you okay?"

"No. Yesterday I healed my mum, and this morning I healed your daughter. Now I'm about to destroy my family."

"If you're not back out here in ten minutes. I'm going to be going in there to get you."

"Declan won't hurt me." Even as she spoke the words, she remembered the last conversation they'd had. He had been angry and judgmental. She had never seen him that way, but it had been a mark of something deeper. She frowned, trying to push the thought out of her mind. Ari had put the thought in her mind, and now she couldn't shake it.

"I'm serious, little bird. You might trust him, but I don't. Even so, I'm going to trust you, but I will burst into your grandmother's home like the big bad grizzly to rescue you if I think you're in danger."

"Ruth won't be happy if you break her front door."

"She'll get over it."

Rayna liked the confident way he talked. No nonsense and to the point. She couldn't bring herself to believe that he was right. She didn't want him to be. "I'll talk to him, and I'll make sure the door is unlocked. Just so you don't need to break through it."

Ari stopped her as she was leaving the car. Rayna glanced down at his hand on her wrist. A searing heat traveled up her arm. All the things they had shared played on repeat in her mind. A lot had changed in twenty-four hours. The memory of what they had shared was imprinted on her body and mind.

"I sensed the last time you were in need, but last night was different. If I'm right, Declan is dangerous. Don't play into his hands. I don't want to lose you, Rayna."

Her chest went tight as he looked at her. "It'll be fine. I can protect myself. "She leaned forward, cupping his face, and kissed him. Then she got out of the car.

RUTH'S HOUSE WAS QUIET. IT WASN'T EMPTY. WITH HER NEW senses, she knew her mum was no longer in the attic but was in the kitchen. Ruth was with her, but they weren't alone. Something tickled at the back of her mind. A part of her wanted to get Ari. There was nothing normal about the situation. There should have been noises. Ruth humming, the clattering of cups, or something. She reached behind her to open the door and then she heard an unmistakable click. A gun.

"Welcome home, Rayna."

The voice belonged to a stranger. She glanced up the stairs. A man she'd never seen before sat at the top. Thick black hair, piercing blue eyes. There was a power to him that made her automatically know he was a shifter. "Who are you?"

He stood up and walked down the stairs, the gun trained on her. "I'm a business associate of your uncle." He gestured toward the kitchen. "Please lead the way."

She could push the front door open and get Ari's attention, but he wouldn't be able to reach her in time. Rayna had spent enough hours at the Academy's gun range to recognize a professional when she saw one. A shifter could heal a lot of injuries but definitely not a bullet to the head. She doubted anyone could heal that.

Ten minutes. Ari had said if she hadn't returned, he would come in after her. Could she buy them time?

As she walked into the kitchen, the first thing she noticed was her mum and Ruth sitting at the table. Uncle Declan sat on the counter, a gun in his hands. Her mum and Nan had both tied to their chairs. Her mum was pale, and tired, judging by the black circles underneath her eyes. Her nan was slumped forward in her chair. The only thing that held her in place was the rope around her waist. She wasn't moving.

Ari was right.

The mysterious man jammed the gun against her lower back, guiding her in the direction of one of the free chairs. Rayna didn't move. Instead, she glared at her uncle.

"Why did you kill Dad?"

He didn't even look guilty, just annoyed. "Who told you that?"

"You're not going to deny it?"

"No point. I figured he might tell you but can't figure out why he let you go." His smile widened. "Unless you healed the girl. Did you?"

"You mean, Daisy? What does that have to do with you killing Dad?"

There was a sharp stab of pain against her lower back. "I'm the one who cut the brake lines. It wasn't anything personal, just business, and since you've fulfilled the bargain. Your uncle is going to come into a hell of a lot of money."

Her animal paced inside of her, but at that moment, the feathery animal wouldn't have been much help. There wasn't enough space in the kitchen to move. She really was on the back foot. "That's why he hired you, for the money?"

"Be a good girl and sit down."

"Fuck you." She spat the words. "What's your plan here? Kill us? What do you have to gain by doing any of this?"

Declan flashed her a cold smile. "I owe people money. Nobody was supposed to find out. You were supposed to gain your caladrius the moment the weight of the trauma slammed into you, and then he would take you for what he needed."

"Who would have taken me?"

"The Broker."

The Broker? She recalled Aubrey mentioning the name. Wasn't that the person who had been after the Miklos Bathory books?

"Why would he have wanted me? No, it doesn't matter." He was trying to put her off from asking questions. There was no doubt in her mind if she sat down, she wouldn't be getting out of the room alive. "Why did you kill him?"

He hopped off the counter. "You have no idea what it

was like to live in your dad's shadow. The golden child. The one who couldn't do anything wrong. Then he got the one thing I wanted. The woman I loved. I had to sit quietly on the sidelines for years, but finally, I saw a way to get him out of the picture and make a little bit of money in the process."

Rayna looked at him and then at her mum. Days of not eating hadn't diminished her beauty, but it had weakened her. "You're in love with Mum?"

Disgust crossed her mum's face. It looked like the feelings were one-sided. Declan took a step toward Hiriko. "She dated me first. Then your dad swooped in after one little argument and took her from me. You should still be with me, Hiriko. You know it, and so do I."

She shook her head, and then Rayna heard a click and felt cold steel pressed against the side of her head. Her mum's eyes widened in panic. Rayna knew she should be scared, but at that moment, all she felt was a detachment.

"I argued with him," Rayna said. "Told him there was no way you would hurt Dad. I defended you."

"And you were wrong. You're not a good agent. You can't see something right in front of your face."

She needed to buy a little more time.

"So, you killed Dad so you could have Mum all to yourself?"

"That and the money," Declan corrected. "You were worth a lot."

"Me?" She shook her head, unconvinced.

"You're using me to pay for your debts?"

Declan shrugged. "The Broker—"

She cut him off. "Who's the Broker? Who did you sell me to?"

"Who do you think? I mean, have you met someone new recently? A certain man, intent on seducing you?"

Ari? No, Declan had to be lying. Rayna's head hurt. "Ari is the Broker?"

"Come on, Rayna. It makes sense, even if you don't want to admit it. He'd been searching for a cure for his daughter, and I knew of a way. The little mystery of you never being able to shift always nagged at me. In my travels, I did some research. Talked to experts all over the world, from professors in universities to wise men and women in tiny villages. The consensus was that someone who had some shifter abilities—such as your self-healing—must have a shifter side. It just hadn't awoken. And you know the fastest way to awaken a shifter side? Introduce the human side to some extreme trauma."

The knowledge that her uncle had been researching her condition, only to plot against her and use her father in his disgusting scheme sickened Rayna, though she couldn't tell if it was worse than knowing the man she'd just been with had been part of it all. She was at a loss for words, but it didn't matter as Declan continued.

"Killing Adam did so many things for us—besides just making me rich. It delivered you right to the Broker's hometown, it inflicted trauma deep enough to spark your caladrius shift, and it made Hiriko available to be with me. A few birds, one well-placed stone."

Rayna didn't bother correcting him on what had actually sparked her shift. Not when the man involved, the man she thought was her mate, might not be who she thought he was. Had it all been a lie? If she looked in the driveway, would he still be there, waiting? Or had that been just one more lie he told that somehow got past her new abilities?

How much time had passed? It didn't matter. If Ari was the Broker, he wouldn't be charging in to save them. Rayna would have to figure out how to do that all on her own. She did have one additional question, though. "Did you know he's my mate?"

Declan's eyes widened slightly and twitched then became dead. She smelled the faint whiff of fear that emanated from him. He hadn't had a clue, and this changed things. "It doesn't matter."

"Oh yes it does," Rayna said with a cocky smile, realizing she might have an advantage. "If you kill me, he won't leave you alone. He'll hunt you to the ends of the earth."

"You can't be mates," Declan scoffed, though it was clear he didn't believe his own words. "He lied to you to get you to trust him. Poor mongrel Rayna. You don't have a mate. You believed whatever lie he told you to get you to spread your legs and fall for him. I mean you healed his daughter. He got exactly what he wanted. Now he has no further use for you."

CHAPTER TWENTY-FIVE

Rage built in the pit of his stomach. Ari hadn't given Rayna the ten-minute leeway he had promised her. Instead, he had crept up to the front door and walked in. It might have been a few years since he had been an agent, and he definitely didn't miss being in the field, but the habits had been difficult to break.

He kept himself low to the ground and still. If the group in the kitchen hadn't been caught up in a wave of emotions, one of them might have sensed him. If they did, nobody would mention it. The men had guns; Ari could smell the oil. Did they know how to use them? He would need to take out the man who held a gun to her head. It might be enough to get Declan to back off. Especially if he knew he was outnumbered.

Ari's bear came to the surface. His eyesight became sharper, and strength surged into his muscles. There wasn't enough space to attack in his animal form, but he had training as an agent, learning how to fight and how to use a gun.

There were still ways it could all go wrong. He sensed

the others in the kitchen. Ruth and a scent similar to Rayna's. Her mum. If anything went wrong, people would get hurt.

"Who's the Broker? Who did you sell me to?" He heard Rayna ask, and that made Ari misstep.

"Who do you think?" Declan shot back. "I mean, have you met someone new recently? A certain man, intent on seducing you?"

"Ari is the Broker?"

Well, fuck.

Not that he had the time to think about the possible implications. The conversation continued, but he tuned it out, instead focusing on what needed to be done. Two criminals were in there, armed and dangerous, holding three women hostage. He had an idea of what to expect from Declan—not much, seeing as he wasn't a fighter—but Ari didn't have information on the other man, the one Declan hired to kill Adam. That made him an unknown, and Ari didn't like unknowns.

As to the women and how much they might be able to fight against their attackers? Ruth was the leader of her seal pod, so he wouldn't be surprised if she knew how to fight and defend herself. Hiriko, though, even if she knew how to fight, was weakened from her recent illness and grief.

Rayna had some training from the Academy, but she wouldn't risk getting into a fight if it meant that anyone else would get hurt. That meant Ari needed to focus on getting one of the men out of the equation before anything broke out.

"He got exactly what he wanted from you." Declan's laugh brought Ari's attention back to the words being exchanged.

"You're wrong." This time she sounded uncertain. He hated to hear her talk like that. This was his own fault. He should have made sure Hendrickson had grabbed Declan.

Just take him off the board and make him vanish like he had promised when they first met.

Save her, his bear growled at him.

"You were duped. And how easy to do so, considering you know nothing about shifters. Nothing about mates. So easy to trick someone as naive as you into thinking something as mundane as everyday lust is actually the mating sense."

Ari wanted to trust Rayna wouldn't believe Declan, but there was no guarantee. She knew the truth of Ari's involvement in Adam's death now, and even if she wasn't sure if she believed it, it was still there.

He could make out the shadow of a man's back. His mate was within arm's reach. He couldn't see the gun, but it had to be there.

I'm right here, Rayna. I haven't abandoned you. There has to be a part of you that can sense me.

He clenched his hand into a fist and ignored the stab of pain as his nails cut into his palm. There was no way to know if she experienced his pain like he had hers, but it was all he had.

It wouldn't take long for the others to catch the scent of his blood. His healing ability kicked in but not before a few droplets of blood hit the floor. Then, he darted forward.

There was a gasp of surprise as he knocked the man's gun hand up into the air. A loud bang, and then Rayna darted forward, aiming for her uncle. There wasn't enough space in the kitchen to fight. Rayna collided with her uncle, pushing him through the door, and they disappeared from sight. Ari noted that the door hadn't been fixed since he broke the frame the previous night. A woman who looked a little like Rayna, but with white hair, was struggling against her bindings. The other woman, Ruth, was slumped forward in her chair. Blood dripped down her face. That was why they hadn't smelled his blood.

Ari had to trust Rayna knew what she was doing, so he focused on the mysterious shifter, who looked a little surprised as Ari shoved him against the cabinetry.

"Aren't you sneaky?" the man sneered.

"I don't think we've met."

"Just an interested party. Declan owes my boss money, and I'm just making sure he follows through with the other half-million. I mean he was right, wasn't he? Rayna healed your daughter. You owe him some money."

"Then what are you doing here? I had every intention of forwarding the money."

"Always good to have a plan B and a plan C. I don't want to fight you."

Ari growled. "No, you don't, but you hurt my mate, threatened her family. There's no way you're walking out of here in one piece."

He punched, catching the other man in the mid-chest. The man fell forward, landing with a thud. There was an almighty crack as Ari's boot connected with his chest. He didn't know what kind of shifter the other man was, but crushed ribs would take a while to heal. Ari grabbed the front of his shirt and threw him out of the back door. He had to trust the women would be able to free themselves. Every minute that passed without knowing if Rayna was all right was one too many minutes.

"Hey, Alyce, I'm sorry," Rayna said. "I know it's early over there. Are you able to get in contact with the UK branch to come and collect someone for me? Make that two someones."

He'd discovered Rayna in the garden, her uncle unconscious beneath her. She had him in a weird hold, the gun a few feet away. She looked up as he entered the garden.

"My uncle. He was behind my dad's death. I know it's complicated, but if he stays here, I can't guarantee my grandmother's pod won't kill him. Not that he deserves any mercy. The sooner he's collected, the better for everyone."

Her eyes flickered back in Ari's direction. This was the part where she let FUC know who the Broker was. He always suspected it might come to this eventually. He even accepted it. At least Daisy was healed. He had everything all set up for her—from custody going to Hendrickson to trust funds that would ensure her every last need was taken care of. It was time to pay for all the things he had done to reach this point.

"He mentioned the Broker. No, I don't know who he is."

Ari raised an eyebrow, but she made a point to ignore him. "My location information is in my personnel file. Collect these two from my grandmother's house." She turned the phone off and looked at Ari.

"It's true, isn't it? You're the Broker."

"I am."

She closed her eyes and groaned, rubbing the bridge of her nose. "You couldn't have lied to me?"

"What would be the point of that? You're one of the shifters with the ability to detect a lie."

"Could Alyce, when I told her I didn't know who the Broker was?"

"Unlikely. There are several traits a shifter reads, but a big one is the scent. Why didn't you tell them who I was?"

"I should have."

"Put these on him." The woman who looked a lot like Rayna walked into the garden. In her hands, she held a set of handcuffs. They weren't like a standard set. The metal was heavier, indicating they were made for shifters.

Ari took them from her and then approached Rayna, who watched him warily. The look broke his heart. He knew the trust they had built had shattered. He owed her a lot, and he never wanted to hurt her. He handed the cuffs to her, and she attached them to her uncle's wrists. Ari walked over to the still unconscious form of Declan's accomplice and put a set on him.

"You must be Hiriko?" Ari said, turning back to the woman once he'd finished.

Rayna's mum nodded. "And you're the Broker."

"I prefer Ari."

"You better get out of here," Rayna said from her place on the ground. "I won't tell them who you are, but there's no guarantee that Declan won't mention something."

The corner of his mouth twitched. "I'm not worried about him. Will I see you again?"

"I'm returning to the Academy. Tell Daisy I said goodbye."

The thought of never seeing her again hurt him on a level he hadn't experienced in years. He didn't want to lose her. "Rayna…"

"How's Ruth?" she asked her mum, pointedly ignoring him again.

"Her healing ability has kicked in. She's going to be okay. You found out the truth, didn't you?" She glanced up at Ari. "About Declan?"

"Yes, I'm sorry for your loss. It doesn't mean much, but I had nothing to do with what happened to your husband. Declan saw an opportunity and took it. I was as much in the dark about it as you were."

"Ari, you need to leave," Rayna said again. Her voice might have been more forceful this time, but it still wavered.

"I'm not going anywhere. I've spent years with one goal in mind, and that was to heal Daisy. With her saved, there's only one thing left to do. I'm going to pay for my crimes."

RAYNA HADN'T KNOWN HOW EVERYTHING WAS GOING TO END. FUC came in and took Declan and his accomplice, and then Ari turned himself in as well. She hadn't been sure if she'd ever see him again. There had also been an awkward encounter with her mum's parents. They had been thrilled Rayna's animal had awoken but all she could remember was the disgust on their faces when they thought she wasn't good enough. Even her mum had been guarded and Rayna suspected there wouldn't be many family dinners in the near future. In the end, she returned to FUCN'A and continued her training.

As expected, representatives from ASS had shown up, demanding Rayna leave BC and go with them to the aerie in Australia to train and then work for them. Alyce Cooper said the decision was up to Rayna, and Rayna chose FUCN'A. The ASS agents weren't happy, but they also weren't about to argue with the infamous llama.

Rayna was given bonus points toward her accreditation for her investigation of her dad's case, as well as the apprehension of the criminals. Then, after she completed all of the shifter courses she'd previously been unable to participate in, she graduated. When they handed her the envelope that contained her apprenticeship assignment, she nearly passed out from shock. Her first field mentor would be the one and only legendary Miranda Brownsmith!

The sabertoothed-bunny shifter was a unique blend of beautiful and crazy in the best kind of way. Everyone liked Miranda. She was impossible to dislike. And Rayna couldn't have received any better training in the field.

In all that time, she never forgot Ari, though. The day she had left him weighed heavily on her mind. She thought about asking Alyce or Miranda what had happened to him, but she hadn't. She had enough to sort through already.

Lying. Manipulating. Saving the lives of people Rayna loved. Her head had been a mess for a long time. She couldn't forget the two main truths, though. Ari was her mate, and everything he'd done had been in an effort to save his daughter.

Despite having no word from Ari, she did hear from Daisy. She'd felt bad, knowing the little girl had lost her mother and now lost her father, too.

The little bear shifter wasn't brilliant with writing, but Rayna suspected Henny helped her with the letters. At first, they mostly wrote about books and Daisy's teddy bears, but after Daisy entered nursery school, she began to tell Rayna all about her new friends.

Rayna couldn't have been happier that she'd helped the little girl get there.

The day she finished her apprenticeship, there was an informal ceremony to mark her official entry into FUC as a full agent. Ruth and Hiriko had wanted to be at the event, but Rayna promised they'd do their own celebration when she returned to the UK the next day. They'd have plenty of time, since she was finally taking a few weeks of leave.

That was why she ended up back in the airport where she had first met Ari.

The bartender was new, but the delayed schedule wasn't.

"What can I get you?" the woman asked.

Even if Rayna hadn't noticed the way the woman's eyes widened as she looked at the stranger approaching, Rayna would have sensed Ari as he walked up behind her. She didn't turn to face him. It had been a full year. She didn't know the first thing to say.

"Two glasses of whiskey."

As soon as his familiar voice hit her ears, she shivered. Her caladrius woke inside of her, stirring to life. Every part of her had missed the bear shifter.

The bartender frowned, realizing they hadn't walked in together, but Rayna nodded. "Sounds good, thanks."

The stool next to her was pulled out, and Ari sat. The first time she ever laid eyes on him, he had worn a suit, not a strand of hair out of place. Tonight, he looked different. Relaxed was the wrong word. His hair was slightly over-grown, falling in front of his dark eyes. He wore a pair of jeans and a sweater—dark green, which suited him. The whole look made him seem more approachable, and she wanted to reach out to him, but it wasn't that easy.

"How did you know I was going to be here?"

"You mentioned to Daisy you were thinking about visiting your mum. It's been a year since your dad passed. It didn't take much of a mental leap to figure out you planned to see Ruth as well."

"Clever."

The bartender put the glasses down, and Ari tapped his card against the payment machine. Rayna took a sip, her throat suddenly dried. Had it really been a year since she last saw him? She wanted to face him, take in his profile, feel his jaw underneath her hand, that sinful mouth under her fingertips. Need twisted in the pit of her stomach.

"If you didn't want me to find you, you wouldn't have mentioned anything to Daisy."

"Daisy and I write to each other about what's going on. This just happened to be what was going on."

He leaned forward. The heat from his body somehow transferred to hers, leaving a trail of goosebumps across her skin. "That is dangerously close to a lie, little bird. I've paid for my mistakes. I've even been a good boy and started using my shadow network for good. What more do you want from me?"

"I want it all to be simple."

He sighed. "That's the one thing I can't give you. I heard what happened with Declan."

Twenty years in a secure prison, one built for shifters. It wasn't enough. Whatever he planned to do when he was released, he wouldn't be able to return to the UK. Ruth had banished him. Every seal pod knew what he did. They knew he wasn't to be trusted. Seals were social animals. He would have to survive without it.

"It's not enough," Rayna whispered. "Dad wouldn't want us to hold a grudge, but even he had his limits. That asshole killed him."

"The day Declan is released he'll have a big target on his back. He owes a lot of dangerous people a ton of money. They aren't going to forget that."

She raised her glass, and Ari clinked his against hers. "I won't lose any sleep over it."

"I'm sorry," he said, finally.

She offered a bitter laugh. "That could cover a wide range of things."

"I'm sorry I deceived you when we first met. I'm sorry I planned on going along with Declan's scheme without learning the specifics of his plan. I'm sorry your dad died for—"

"Declan murdered my dad for his own selfish reasons. You just happened to be involved, but had you not been, I guarantee he would have killed him anyway." She'd spent a lot of time thinking about it and always came to the same conclusion. "You needed your daughter healed, but you're not the only one out there. Had it not been you, he would have found someone else and done exactly the same thing."

Ari sighed, and she sensed some amount of weight had been lifted from him with her words. "Still. I'm sorry. For all of it."

"I've already forgiven you for all that," she said, glancing at him and finding herself getting lost in his deep eyes. "I had to so I could move forward with my life without carrying the weight of all that."

"I see." He nodded slightly, and she couldn't read his expression.

"You're heading back home?" she asked, changing the subject.

He nodded. "I had a special meeting with the FUC."

"You did? What did they say?"

He reached into his inside pocket and pulled out a lanyard. He nudged it toward her. She frowned but picked it up. Rayna had seen plenty of them when she visited headquarters. "They offered you a job?" She ran her fingers over the lanyard. It wasn't fake.

"Only once I'd spent this past year making reparations and proving I'm reformed. They weren't happy with me, but they understood why I took a dark path. How the weight of Becca's loss drove me away from FUC and how my desperation to save Daisy drove me to do reprehensible things. I'm also going to be spending a lot of time with a therapist. Can't say I'm looking forward to that."

"And they're giving you another chance?"

"That they are." Ari glanced up. The bartender was now on the other side of the bar. "I never told you what happened to her—Becca. I was on assignment, but my cover was blown. They grabbed Becca. Used her to torture me. They pumped me full of drugs so I couldn't shift." He rolled the glass between his hands. "Then they shot her in the head."

Rayna could hear the pain in his voice. The loss of his wife still weighed heavily on his mind. It likely would for the rest of his life. "I'm sorry."

"Becca was my tech support. She should have been safe, but they grabbed her on the way home. That was when I decided I couldn't live the life anymore."

"And now you're working with them again."

"The other option was a jail cell, where agents would be able to visit and consult with me on cases. This way I'll be around when Daisy grows up. I'll also be here for you."

"You know I plan on being an active agent."

"And part of that will kill me, but I'm not going to dictate how you lead your life, Rayna." He reached across and touched her hand. They laced their fingers together. "You're my mate, Rayna. I love you with all my heart."

She looked at the perfect way their hands linked together, his tan against her pale skin. The simple touch made her heart race. If she went with what her animal wanted, they would find the nearest hotel room. Rayna did her best to ignore the persistent voice in her head. She wasn't in a rush to get her heart broken. Trusting him wasn't going to be easy. Ari's whole life was based on secrets and half-truths. "One day at a time."

"I can live with that." He tugged her closer, and her breath caught. Being this close, she could see the flecks of dark gold in his eyes. "Can I kiss you?"

She smiled. "I think I can live with that." She echoed his words as he sealed their love with a kiss.

The End.

Or is it? There are more FUC Academy books from other authors coming your way soon!

To find out more about these books and more, visit worlds.EveLanglais.com or sign up for the EveL Worlds newsletter. If you haven't already downloaded the **free Academy intro** (written by Eve Langlais) make sure you grab it at worlds.evelanglais.com/wordpress/book/fucacademy1!

This mouse is about to receive the lion's share of adventure...

Aubrey Taylor dreamed of becoming an international superspy, but her parents warned that a mouse shifter wasn't meant for such risky professions. Instead, she became a librarian for FUCN'A, though she never dreamed it would see her off on the experience of a lifetime.

Jackson Holt, lion shifter and famed agent is facing a foe more powerful than any FUC enemy… his mother. She wants her alpha son to assume his position as leader of their pride, but he wants to save the world, one mission at a time.

When he swings by the academy to thank Aubrey for her assistance on a case, he inadvertently brings danger to her door. Between shots fired, jaguar assassins, and a lioness mother who will never accept her son with a mouse, Jackson has his work cut out for him.

__Buy Now!__

This sly fox is eyeing a score, but a handsome wolf is blocking her.

Lizzie has always lived outside the shifter world, taking on jobs that allowed her to sneak around unnoticed. But when her sister is threatened, she joins FUCN'A.

Wolf shifter Neil is adjusting to life as a solo agent, and fate has a surprise in store for him when his mate sits next to him on his international flight. Lizzie is sweet and sexy, but she's hiding something and he's determined to sniff it—and her—out.

Lizzie knows an agent like Neil couldn't be serious about someone like her. Especially when he learns how she's used him to gain access to the Academy.

Can the crafty fox keep the wolf at bay, or will he howl his way into her heart before it's too late?

Buy Now

Samantha Allard has always wanted to be a writer. She spent her teenage years reading books and scribbling notes on napkins. Now she's older, perhaps not any wiser, and getting her stories published. Young adult, steampunk or fantasy. The genre doesn't matter as long as the story is told.

She can be found in her office most days. Others she trapped at the dreaded day job.